Bristol Short Story Prize Anthology

Volume Three

BRIST⊕L

First published in 2010 by Bristol Review of Books Ltd,
Unit 5.16 Paintworks, Bath Rd, Bristol BS4 3EH

1

ISBN: 9780955955549

Cover designed by Gaby Selby
Set in Adobe Garamond
Layout designed by Dave Oakley, Arnos Design, Bristol
Printed and bound in Great Britain by Short Run Press,
Exeter, Devon

www.bristolprize.co.uk
www.brbooks.co.uk

Contents

Introduction

Welcome to the third Bristol Short Story Prize Anthology. The BSSP is now established as a short story competition of national significance. We still remain modest about our international importance, even though we had entrants from more than 30 non-UK countries this year.

What makes the competition so enjoyable is the writers. They recognise, and some relish, that the BSSP welcomes short stories of all styles, genres and lengths; the length of stories this year varied from the top of our word limit- 3,000- to 300 words.

Judging this year's 1,500 entries was no easy task as we received an impressive range of submissions. Some popular themes emerged from the long list, particularly motherhood, and for some reason *feet* cropped up in many of the stories. Non-linear narratives were plentiful this year and the number of flash fiction submissions also increased. Flash fiction challenges pre-conceived ideas on structure, narrative and in some cases many established views on what exactly a short story is. We were pleased to find that the criteria we used to judge the stories stood up to the challenge of comparing the more traditional well-crafted and well-told stories with work that was more experimental in style and structure. The quality of all submissions in the long list shows that the written word and the short story in particular, are as vibrant and exciting as they have ever been. Writers continue to discover innovative and creative ways to challenge and push the format, ways that both capture the imagination and touch the emotions of readers. There is a story for everybody in this anthology.

As judges we were looking for tales that were well-told, and stories that drew us into their world and felt complete; stories that did not leave you wanting more or made you feel you had not had enough. We were also looking for stories that had one other quality as well, but more on that later. Personal taste, obviously, comes into the judging process, but with five judges from different backgrounds, all with different tastes, the writers could not write to a formula to win and the innovation, creativity and craft in the long list impressed all of us. Which brings me to the last quality of a short story and something that stood out in the entries we were lucky enough to read; in re-reading and discussing the stories we frequently discovered different elements and more qualities within them, surely one of the tell-tale signs of great writing.

My thanks to fellow judges and muffin eaters Joe Berger, Maia Bristol, Helen Hart and Tania Hershman for bringing such commitment and passion to the task. And thanks, too, to the dedicated team of readers who diligently and resolutely select the long list – Sophie Collard, Katherine Hanks, Lu Hersey, Richard Jones, Mike Manson, Dawn Pomroy, Ali Reynolds and Keith Taylor. Also, big thanks to Joe Melia who is a great champion for BSSP and provides a solid base from which the Bristol Short Story Prize will grow. He is already putting plans into action for next year that will engage the next generation of readers with short stories.

Thanks, also, to Chris Hill, Jonathan Ward, Gary Embury and the final year Illustration students at the University of the West of England. It's always a joy to work with such an inspirational group of people and we look forward to seeing Gaby Selby's great cover design in many bookshops.

And finally, but most importantly, many thanks to all those who sent in their wonderful stories - it has been a great pleasure to read them.

Bertel Martin (Chair of the judging panel)

Judges' profiles

Maia Bristol

Maia Bristol is UK Sales Manager at Faber and Faber, a role that gives her the opportunity to champion not only the independent publishing of Faber but also the nine other publishers Faber represent - which include Canongate, Atlantic and Granta. This role has given her vast experience in spotting innovative and original writing talent, a part of her work she really relishes. Maia is also a gifted translator with a specialism in fiction. She lives with her family in the Westbury-on-Trym area of Bristol and is currently enjoying maternity leave in Austria.

Tania Hershman

Passionate about short stories, Tania Hershman - whose first collection, *The White Road and Other Stories*, was commended in the *2009 Orange Award for New Writers* - founded *The Short Review* in 2007 to shine the spotlight on short story collections and their authors. Originally from London, Tania, a former science journalist, recently moved to Bristol with her partner after spending 15 years in Jerusalem, Israel. Her award-winning stories and flash fiction have been published online and in print and broadcast on Radio 4. Tania is currently writer-in-residence in Bristol University's Faculty of Science. Her website is www.taniahershman. com and she blogs about writing at www.titaniawrites. blogspot.com

Bertel Martin (Chair)

Bertel Martin is a co-editor of *Bristol Review of Books* magazine and director of City Chameleon, a company that specialises in publishing poetry and producing live literature performances. The process includes writer development and support, creating access to print for community groups and voluntary organisations and partnership working. Prior to setting up City Chameleon, Bertel has worked as a writer, performer, arts administrator and arts project manager in literature, dance, and theatre in professional, community and education environments. He is also currently on the Board of Trustees for Circomedia, part of the steering group for the Sustained Theatre SW hub (to raise the profile of Black and Minority Ethnic theatre practitioners), http://www.citychameleon.co.uk

Helen Hart

Helen Hart has been a published author since 1999. She has written a number of novels under pseudonyms for Scholastic, Virgin Books and HarperCollins, and has been a regular contributor to Emap Magazines' *FHM*. As a co-director of Redwing Design, she supplies copywriting, editing and proofreading services for commercial clients. In 2007 Helen became the founding director of Bristol-based publisher SilverWood Books.

Joe Berger

Joe Berger is a Bristol-based author, cartoonist, illustrator and animator. He has written and illustrated several picture books for Puffin, including *Bridget Fidget* and the sequel, *Bridget Fidget Hold on Tight!* He also co-writes and draws a single panel cartoon about food in *the Guardian* weekend magazine, with his long-time collaborator Pascal Wyse. Joe and Pascal have created several award-winning animated shorts, and a Bafta and Emmy nominated title sequence for the BBC drama Hustle. Joe lives in the Montpelier district of Bristol with his wife and their three daughters.

1ˢᵗ Prize
Valerie O'Riordan

Valerie O'Riordan grew up in Dublin, Ireland, and studied English and Philosophy at Trinity College, Dublin. She moved to the UK in 2004 and spent several years working as a video editor for the BBC in Birmingham before throwing in the televisual towel in 2009 to head north to Manchester and get her MA in Creative Writing. She's been writing seriously since 2008 and she's a member of the Fiction Forge writing group. Her recent publication credits include *elimae* and *Litro*, and in 2009 she was a finalist in the inaugural *Flatmancrooked Fiction Prize*. She's currently working on her first novel.

Mum's the Word

Three times with his grunting and the calloused hand over my mouth: first, the kitchen wall rough at my back; second, hands and knees against the splintered attic floor; third, pushing me into the thin mattress, while my mother slept in the next room, her belly swollen and taut. Then a sticky wrap of silver paper, chocolate to slip into my pocket on the way to school. Hands and legs all sticky, and neither of us speaking.

When the time came, they rammed a tongs between my mother's legs, but all they got out was a tangled grey-face thing that took a single half-hearted breath. My mother was split open. I heard her screaming. Later I helped my aunts boil the bedsheets: we scoured and bleached them, but finally they sent me out to dump them in the skip in the back alley. I bundled the rest up too, the stained knickers and the ripped tights, wrapped them up in the pillowcase where nobody would see. I crouched in the dark beside the metal bin and vomited, a watery spew all over my good shoes. He was watching me from the kitchen window when I came back up the path, my hand on my stomach. He said, it's the two of us now, girl, and held me by the shoulder. His face was red and wet.

When I couldn't go to school anymore, the clothes straining to cover me, my armpits stained with the sweat of my bulk, he left me alone. My shadow on the bedroom wall in the moonlight was like the moon itself, round and still. I heard him coming in when the light was trickling over the treetops, his steps back and forth in the corridor, his sobbing through the wall. My aunts had stopped visiting when he stopped letting them inside; I sweated and pushed on my own, and the baby screamed. He had it brought away; the social worker shook her head as she swaddled it and said love, a big girl like you, didn't you take precautions? His arm around my shoulder, fingers kneading, as he said, I'll keep a better eye on her, Miss, don't you worry.

2nd Prize
Ian Madden

Ian Madden's short fiction has appeared in several anthologies including the *Bridport Prize* and the inaugural volume of the *Bristol Short Story Prize Anthology*. He lives in Edinburgh.

Only the Sure of Foot

The baker's house stood solitary and white at the foot of the mountain. Its remoteness made his wife's nightly trek all the more remarkable. When she was sure her husband was asleep, she would take down the dog's lead and prise open the door.

Some men came back from the trenches with scars or behaved differently, wildly. The baker returned with eyebrows bleached by the sun and an even greater proneness to tidiness and order than before the Kaiser's troublemaking. Compared to some of the tales his wife had heard, an overly neat house and hearth didn't seem too high a price to pay to have her husband back.

The baker had always felt shame at his meticulousness. He believed it to be unmanly, a weakness. Like a limp or a lisp. His wife had never mentioned what she couldn't but notice: the unfailingly precise position of everything in their home, especially the newspaper. Timing and precision were usually the preoccupations of slighter, weedier men but the Baker Munro was taller and broader than any man on the island. Many of his quiet insistences took place at work where it was easy to regard them as no more than doing a thorough job. Saving things, not throwing anything away, was one of his tenets. It was different with the offcuts. These imperfections had to be disposed of immediately. This he left to his wife. And dispose of them she did – though not in a manner that would have met with her husband's approval.

Between the steady rhythms of snores rattling the walls – before they progressed to the four-to-the-bar snorts during which her husband practically chomped himself awake – the baker's wife would get up and put on her clothes. When she first started to do this, every garment had seemed cumbrous and unhelpful. But in time she got used to dressing almost without breathing.

Downstairs everything was prepared. The dog knew not to bark. She took down from the peg the strip of seal skin which served as a leash. This was by way of preparation, anticipation, as there was never any need for the leash; not with such an intelligent creature. Each of the four successive dogs the couple had owned had been given the name Buchal – Gaelic for 'shepherd.' As his mistress and he were about to set off, the current collie became excited but quietly so; he had witnessed his master's temper. Once outside, Buchal led the way.

Never one for words, the Baker Munro wouldn't speak if a grunt would do. The only baker on the island, he knew that – especially in gathering season – crofters and their womenfolk had work enough to do without attempting their own baking or catching the steamer (their only choices if they didn't buy bread from him). His prices reflected this.

With the war over all the talk had been of bright days ahead, of getting back to normal. But normal was the last thing many islanders wanted. They'd have preferred having enough to eat. A lot were faring worse than during the fighting. Darroch, the baker's best friend during boyhood (and the most freckled man on the island) now had five children. But he had married a woman whose family lived on a neighbouring island. This family had – long before the baker was born – had a rift with the Munros. The baker couldn't even stand to have the other island mentioned.

'The children call me "auntie."' That was all she said. Years ago.

The baker reacted as if she had admitted adultery.

Darroch's family occupied a crumbling house by the Sound, on the very edge of the island near where the land was ripped, fallen – not meant for humans. They lived in need so dire it made the baker's wife not only mention them in her prayers but made her question who or what she was praying to.

Her nocturnal errand began in spring on a night of hardly any darkness. The baker's wife strode all the way to the Shale-Cut Wall. There were a good many shale-cut walls on the island but the northern perimeter of Sheppey's Field was known as the Shale-Cut Wall – as if there was just the one. It was at this spot that she handed over the package wrapped in sacking. The walks continued throughout the summer nights but by the middle of autumn the slopes became rougher; wind and water combined to dissuade her not from venturing out, but from waiting around. So the baker's wife decided she would have to leave the packages somewhere where they'd be safe from rain and cormorants until they were collected. There was only one place she could think of.

It tired and upset her, her husband's ability to harbour ill will against members of a family simply because they were just that: members of a family. The baker kept his grievance burnished and full of hot coals, as if such a constant temperature might be beneficial; grievance a kind of bed warmer. Certain tribes are predisposed to it, she knew. It was practically in their pigmentation. Pride in a longstanding feud – the kind in which grudges became heirlooms – seemed to her much more shameful than the perennial urge to tidy up.

The reason for the feud had never been put into words. For all she knew, it could have been something as piffling as an argument between great-grandfathers over a hay rake. Had its cause been spoken of, the wrath which kindled the breach might have lost some of its glow. The baker's determination to cling to an ancestral wrong only increased his wife's determination not to.

Sheppey's Field ended in a jagged rim of cliff. Kittiwakes and guillemots nested on these sudden ledges of rock. Half-way between this cliff and the nearest road the land was divided by a deep cleft. Precipitous and craggy, the sides were so steep that a person would have to be agile and determined in order to clamber down to the bottom. They'd have to be even more agile and determined to climb back up. Among the crevices and rubble was a big black cauldron. Stories abounded as to how such a story-book object had come to be there. But no one knew for certain. It was one of the island's mysteries.

The cauldron looked as if it had once belonged in the kitchen of a great house, one where a banquet could be prepared. It didn't look particularly worn out. The lid was still with it; which was surprising – or perhaps not.

Who, even if they had a use for a cauldron lid, could have carried it back from such terrain? Anyone wanting to make off with it would have needed the strength of five and a sturdy cart waiting way up on what flat there was. So the cauldron stayed put, wondered at, for longer than the oldest inhabitant could remember.

The baker's wife kept up her secret walk for years. Nothing stopped her, not sleet, snow, driving rain. Nor the howling gales which would have blown a lantern in a circle had she taken one with her. But there were also swathes of calm, times when there was such completeness and variety of light that it seemed as though darkness and savageries of winter were being made up for. On one such night she saw a pair of stray puffins over by the cliff edge. They must have somehow become separated from the colony that lives on an island miles and miles to the west. She desperately wanted to tell someone this. But didn't. It was enough that Buchal, too, had seen the lost birds.

No matter what the weather, the baker's wife was always back in time to have her husband's breakfast ready.

There came a night early one autumn – not long after she'd seen the puffins - when the baker's wife hadn't the strength to cross the room let alone make the journey to Sheppey's Field. She felt listless and weepy. Reluctantly, her husband went to fetch old MacCuish. After his wife had been examined and the visit and medicine paid for, the baker accompanied the doctor to the door.

'It's the change of life, nothing more,' assured MacCuish.

Glancing back at the door they had just come through, the Baker Munro whispered, 'Is it catching?'

A bitter squall stung the fingers and frowns of those standing respectful and suspended on the kirkyard's narrow path. One of the mourners detached himself from his wife and children and approached the widower. The baker heard his first name. Darroch and the baker stood before each other. Along with everyone else on the island, Darroch had heard about how the old doctor had been of the opinion that nothing much had been the matter.

Three older children stood by their mother. Two small boys hung behind Darroch, rueful. Even their lips were freckled. Their father looked at the sandy eyebrows. He would have liked to tell about crossing those miles to Sheppey's Field then edging his way down to where only the sure of foot could venture and collecting the burlap parcels from inside the old cauldron. But these marches had only been necessary because of the baker. So no, Darroch would not mention the offcuts which had kept his family alive. The thanks belonged to the dead woman. Even the night before her death, the packages had been in their usual place.

'She was a strong woman,' Darroch said. 'Strong to the end.'

The Baker Munro nodded.

Darroch was not to know what only the doctor and the baker himself knew; that for her last few days the baker's wife had been too weak to leave her bed. And the widower would never tell of the dawns when he'd come downstairs to find the dog's leash hanging the wrong way round on the peg. Nor would he mention how Buchal – tongue lolling sideways with the pleasure of it – had bounded to the byre and stood panting by what looked like a nose-bag. It was beyond him to speak of the open spaces traversed those final nights; nights when, after the doctor had made his solemn visit, the baker – once he was sure the morphine was working – had donned his thickest clothes and strode out.

The children in the kirkyard watched to see who would say what.

But words could be as treacherous as wet rocks at the bottom of a ravine.

The Baker Munro was at a loss as to how to convey that there'd no longer be any need for the long walk, the climb. No more hauling aside the cauldron lid. Their faces numbed by the cold, the two men struggled to keep their footing as they stumbled from word to word.

3rd Prize
Rachel Howard

Rachel Howard has an MA in Creative Writing from Sussex University. She has two daughters, and is a singer in an eleven-piece jive swing band, amongst other things. She was born in Sheffield but now lives in Brighton. She is currently writing a collection of short stories set in the south of Spain. This is her first published work.

Gardening

It started in March. The smell of lavender in my garden reminded me of the hospital room where my mum died, a stick in your throat bleach smell they insisted on topping up every four hours. A few weeks later in April the weather should have been warming up, but my breath was still turning to smoke when I went out, and I felt shivery, wanting to stick to the edges of the pavement, as far away from the road as possible. As I was walking back from the shops one evening, a car zoomed past me on the zebra crossing, missing me by centimetres. The neon lights from the restaurants across the road made my eyes hurt, and I thought I saw rats chewing at the bags of rubbish lying in front of them. After that I stopped going out into the street. I couldn't even step into the garden, and now I can't think about being outside without imagining myself frozen on a street corner, unable to make my way home.

I used to spend hours in my garden, listening to the insects crawling through dead leaves, staring up at the ash trees by the fence that make the house invisible from the road. It's a wild garden, overgrown in summer with giant daisies and hollyhocks. The willow tree is as tall as the house; the fronds flounce in the wind and tap on my window, waking me up. In spring, its leaves are acid green. In summer, they turn the colour of olives.

And now that I no longer inhabit the outside world, an old woman has taken up residence in my garden. She won't come into the house. She prefers to sleep under the skirts of the willow tree, wrapped in blankets, lying on cardboard. When I first saw her I thought she was a man, an old tramp or street drinker who had wandered in looking for a place to sleep. I felt scared, on my own in a house that can't be seen from the road, but she rolled over and revealed her face, a dream skirting across her forehead. She woke up blinking, her eyes rimmed with red. I made her a cup of tea, opened the window and put it on the ledge. She sat up and smiled at me, rubbing her back with one hand and picking the leaves out of her hair with the other. When she spoke, her voice was hoarse; I couldn't understand her language. She pointed to herself and said, 'Elena.' I beckoned her into the house; she shook her head. I spoke my name, and she repeated it over and over again.

Elena stayed another night under the tree. In the morning, I opened the window and we conversed again in our different languages. Her words are elongated, with soft endings, Eastern European I imagine, Hungarian, Polish, maybe Croatian. She could be sixty, or sixty-five. Sometimes when she walks, it's like she's carrying a sack of coal on her back. She wears layers of black clothing, and her hair is matted, tied up in a bun.

Elena has remained in the garden. Occasionally I see her disappear out of the gate, but she always comes back, and I'm glad when she does. If it weren't for seeing her face every day, I might just stay in bed and never get up.

Spring is advancing, and there hasn't been much rain. The garden is withering. I sit in an armchair with the stuffing leaking out underneath it, staring at the damp patterns in the ceilings, trying to remember what my mum looked like when she was young, standing outside the school gates, laughing with the other mums.

Elena finds the outside tap, and waters the garden with a hosepipe. I open the window; I can almost hear the roots of the plants sucking up water. She collects leaves, twigs, weeds, and bits of rubbish, tidying them into piles. She leaves the garden for a long time, returning with an old picture frame the size of a hardback book and two bags of empty beer cans. She stamps on the cans, crushing them flat, then piles them up, six in each pile. These she places in a semi-circle around the trunk of the willow tree. She pulls out a photo from her pocket, fixes it into the frame with tape, and leans it against the tree, in the middle of the cans. The photo is a black and white picture of two young men. They both have curly hair, and are smiling. Elena sits staring at the photo. She puts two candles in front of it, pushing them into the soil. As dusk gathers into the garden, she lights the candles. The flames flicker shadows across the faces.

I call to Elena and beckon her into the house but she holds her palm up to me and turns back to her photograph. When it is fully dark I close the window. Now I can only see my own reflection in the glass. I move closer and peer out. Elena has fallen asleep next to the shrine she has made, the candles have blown out.

The next day I leave a bucket of hot water for her on the window ledge. She disappears amongst the bushes to wash. From somewhere she gets food. Bread, cheese, apples and oranges. She pushes some fruit through the open window, pointing at my stomach.

In the winter a couple lived with me in the house. They had stuff on every surface. Empty wine bottles, magazines, wool, glue, apples, a goldfish in a bowl. They watched telly constantly, and talked through the programmes. I snapped one day and shouted at them to shut up and turn it off. The woman, Georgia, said I was weird. They left and went travelling. They always bought large amounts of food, sacks of potatoes and onions, tins of vegetables, which they didn't take with them. Now this is all I have to eat, apart from what Elena gives me.

At night I lie awake listening to the London traffic. The only time it becomes quiet outside is between four and five in the morning. This is the dead time, when everything stops, like the moment a swing reaches the top of its arc, before it plunges back down to the ground. During this lull, this hush before everything starts up again, I imagine a field outside, grasses blowing, a pond with sleeping ducks.

Elena is still here. A large amount of her time is spent sitting under the willow tree staring at her shrine or tidying up the garden. She mimes war to me, bombs, planes and people dying. I know her shrine must be to her sons. I wonder if she has anybody here, in London; I want to go and help her find them, but I know I can't open the front door, step out of the house and into the street.

My family and friends think I'm in South America. I've unplugged the phone, and hide in the bathroom at the back of the house if anyone knocks on the door. Elena hides too; I've seen her from my bedroom window, crouching amongst the brambles at the side of the house.

My ex-boyfriend Joe sends me a letter. We were together for five years, until I grew an invisible barrier around my body. Three months ago - February the fifteenth - was the last time we had sex. His skin felt like cardboard, and the way he smelt was different. Afterwards he said, 'I can't be with you if you treat me this way, like someone you don't even like.'

'I can't treat you any other way,' I said, and rolled away from him. He jumped out of bed, and into his clothes. He slammed the front door so hard I heard plaster scatter onto the floor.

On the back of the envelope he has written in red pen 'PLEASE FORWARD THIS TO ALICE IN BRAZIL - I DON'T HAVE HER ADDRESS.'

As I read the letter, I imagine him, sitting opposite me on the sofa. His hair would be sticking up, like he'd just woken up. He'd ask me about my art, what I was doing in my studio, and I would say to him that I've given it up, because the thought of leaving the house gives me cramps in my stomach. My poor baby he'd say and hug me, but then he'd say you have to stop dwelling on everything Alice, it's been a year since she died. He'd use his softest voice to try and coerce me into pulling myself together. Instead of replying to him I sit in my armchair and write a letter to my mum, telling her all the things I never told her when she was alive.

The days get hotter. Elena talks to me through the open window, using her hands. I'm unhealthy she says, pointing at my pale face. She goes out of the garden, and returns with a bag full of lettuce, spinach, beans and tomatoes. I make salad for us, and a cup of tea. She likes it strong with no milk. After we have eaten, I play music for her, salsa, swing, rock-and-roll. She dances, stiffly at first, but then she starts twirling her hips, and for the first time I see her smile. I dance too, she mirrors my movements, but she won't come in, and I stay in my house, missing my garden.

I stop listening to the traffic, and sleep at least twelve hours a night, going to bed at nine or ten. One night I dream I am standing on a beach in darkness watching the sweeping beam of a lighthouse. I turn slowly, following the light's progress. A wailing noise breaks into my sleep, forcing me awake. The light is outside in the street flashing on and off. I put on my jeans and rush downstairs. Through the window I can see two policemen holding Elena, one on each arm. She is crying. I bang on the window. 'What are you doing to her? Leave her alone.'

'It's alright miss, we caught her in your garden, trying to break into your house,' one of them shouts, and shakes Elena's arm.

I hoist up the window. 'She sleeps in the garden, she's not a burglar.'

'A neighbour called us,' says the taller policeman. 'We'll just get her in the van and I'll come and take your details.'

'No, leave her. I don't mind her being here.'

They pretend they can't hear me and drag Elena out from under the willow tree, becoming tangled in the fronds, swearing. She resists them but she is like a fledgling bird out of its nest. She looks back over her shoulder at me as they pull her towards the gate.

I can't get enough air in my lungs, but I force myself to twist the catch on the door and pull it towards me. The trees flash blue and white. 'Stop!' I shout. 'Don't arrest her, she wasn't trying to break in.'

The policemen turn around, still holding Elena. I walk out of the door and up the path. My face stings with the freshness of the outside air. I can smell damp grass, and exhaust fumes. 'I know it sounds funny, but she sleeps in my garden.'

'Your neighbours next door saw her trying to break in.'

'She wouldn't try and get into the house, she never has, and she's been here for weeks. '

The taller policeman wipes his forehead with his sleeve. 'Why would you want an old tramp woman kipping in your garden?'

'It's fine with me. I think she probably has her own house in the area. She's lonely.'

'If you're not bothered about her being here, we'll have to let her go. We'll have to file a report though. It might be against the byelaws.'

The policemen let go of Elena, and brush down their uniforms. They switch off the flashing lights. I hug Elena and lead her back under the tree. Her shrine has been kicked in all directions, the photo is lying face down on the earth. I pick it up, wipe the soil off with my tee shirt and prop it up against the tree. I find her blankets and wrap her up in them. Now I am outside, I have stopped shaking. 'Do you want to come in?' I say, looking towards the house. Elena is still crying, but she smiles at me and brings her hand up to her mouth, like she is drinking.

'You want some tea?'

'Tea,' she says and steps through the front door.

Mike Bonsall

Mike Bonsall is 25. His mother is from Lancashire, his father is from Yorkshire, and they thought it best to raise him on neutral ground in Cumbria. He currently lives in Birmingham, where he works as a conjuror of diabolical spreadsheets, but wants to return to the North and live in a cottage with his girlfriend. He is a sci-fi nut, and although he wants to try writing in some more widely accessible genres, he always ends up throwing a few robots in. Mike hasn't had any writing training but takes advice from friends. This will be his first publication.

Man Friday and the Sockball Championships

Aman wakes up in a prism of light, lying on a cool hard floor, face down. It's a familiar feeling.

He feels the pressure points where his body's uneven distribution of weight has steadily pushed his bones, the concealed hard points within his general volume, through the softer fleshy bits. Those bits ache gently, having been pressed between the rest of his body and the transparent plastic below. Well, it might not be plastic, but he doesn't know any better.

It is not unpleasant for him, these days. For him it's a sensation of being well grounded, of having parts that seem to try harder than others to hug the surface of the prism, a subconscious activity his body gets on with during the night. He feels more substantial in the mornings, whereas by the evening he has eroded somewhat; some days more so than others.

He likes to think of it as a prism of light, when in fact it is a simple empty cube. His grasp of geometry is sufficient to be aware of his error, but there is no-one to correct him, and he fancies that if one day there is, he will relate it as a play on the word prison. Ha ha.

But it does do something with light. Gathers and emits it, somehow. As do the rest of the cubes.

Don't worry about the rest of the cubes just yet, he thinks. That's an afternoon activity.

After lying awake for broadly the right amount of time, he surges up from the ground and collects his clothes, folded on the floor to the right, against the wall of his prism. He dresses with a sense of urgency, putting on everything in the little pile except for his orange body warmer, which he seldom wears, and his socks, which he'll use shortly and will make him slip as he pads softly around the interior of the cube. He does fifty laps but alternates at random, to avoid shortening one leg. This is one of the last superstitions of survival here which he still bothers to hold to.

What thoughts should I have today? He wonders while jogging. Size of the cube? Too easy. Four of my heights plus the distance from foot to just above the knee. Nine metres, with a margin for error of 5cm, unless I've grown at all. I'm thirty, kind of, so not likely.

Here's a good one.

You would think, he recites silently, that the contrast of brightness inside the cube with the relative gloom outside would create a very crisp reflection on the totally clear plastic. But that's not the case; it's very faint. Why should that be? Is there some quality to the light, or to the plastic?

This is a good one, he remembers, because it isn't possible for him to work out the answer. Once, after he had already been here for a very long time, he came to the conclusion that he would be able to continue to improve his body and his mind indefinitely. Certainly he was different by then, more aware of things, surprisingly so given there is far less to be aware of in here.

Now he doesn't believe that anymore.

He lacks reference data. He can't expand his vocabulary, and so cannot keep track of the new things he thinks about unless he makes up new words, which he won't do. He thinks it is too ridiculous. Also, he doesn't have any tools, not even a stick to draw shapes in the sand like an ancient Greek philosopher, who, after all, worked a heck of a lot out from first principles. Or any sand, for that matter.

Today, he decides that the reason his reflection is so ephemeral is that the light doesn't originate from a single defined point inside the prism. It is filled with light like a glowing Chinese lantern, floating in the New Year sky. Except, where the lantern does in fact have a fixed point concealed by opaque parchment, the prism is transparent and the fixed point is absent, or somehow hidden. He knows it isn't really an explanation, as it leads to the even more perplexing question of how that is even possible and why it really has any bearing on the nature of his reflection, but it is the position he most often arrives at in this case. He doesn't continue with the line of enquiry this time, knowing it unlikely to bear much fruit.

He has other thoughts that morning; this is just an example. They are all thoughts he has had before, though. Being unable to improve his brain enough to perceive new things beyond a certain ceiling, to really learn, his cache of speculations has been recycled many times. Original thoughts are few and far between.

After running, he stretches luxuriously for an hour or so, limbering up like an athlete. His body is better than it used to be, though again only up to a point, determined by something on a genetic level he believes. It's tough and strong. It's attractive, or would be if there was someone to attract. He used to be slightly fat, and then, of course, he became very thin in the early days here. Now he's lean.

Next he takes his socks, still lying on the floor, and folds them together in such a way that they form a soft little ball. Ever so carefully, he shifts the weight on his feet to adopt a familiar, well practiced position, and holds the little bundle ahead of himself. His fingers slowly release, and the bundle drops. His foot intercepts it cleanly as he swings round his leg, and the sockball rebounds from the wall of the cube with a barely audible bong. He darts forward and catches it on the right knee, then volleys it once more at the wall. Over and over.

He calls it sockball. This is the semi finals of the 51st championship – he's only ever won the title four times. The wall takes the first set, but once he gets into a rhythm, he barely misses a rebound. He imagines the gentle reverberations echoing out from his prism; one, two, three, bong, bong, bong.

The game ends more quickly than usual, with him the victor. His form is good. He rests, tired but satisfied, idling until the next part of the day.

Finally afternoon does come, or what passes for afternoon; a decision, a feeling that that is what it is, and he allows himself to take in the wider environment. He unties his socks and puts them on, still with much hopping about after all this time. He straightens, and stops focusing on the near at hand, the few objects within his field of vision, the very faint reflections on his prism walls, and he looks out.

He sees endless clear cubes with rounded edges, identical to his, stretching in a line ahead of him. Each is fifty, maybe sixty metres apart, and suspended without any visible means, just like his own. He sees each one through the last, a little glowing square inside a little glowing square inside a little glowing square.

He is floating with them all in a vast cavern, in cross section an ellipse, which proceeds away from him into the distance, ahead and behind. The air is clear in here, and he can see a long way, tens of kilometres. Even so, he can only barely perceive the downward curve of the structure he is in, a perception upon which is based his belief in the giant ring. Maybe he is in space, or maybe this is the curve of a small moon he sees.

There must be thousands of visible cubes, though he sees only a few dozen as individuals before they are points of light within one another, and then a merging glow which drops down with the gradual arc of the floor and goes dim. He thinks how beautiful it is.

All of these other cubes are empty.

The inside edge of this colossal ring is, he judges, some forty metres below him. It is made of continuous parallel bands running longways down the cavern, whereas the walls and the ceiling, really the same surface, are bands which arch over his prism and the other cubes. About twenty metres clearance to the sides, forty metres again above. The structure may be of metal, maybe not; russet in colour.

He thinks about the long bands on the floor, remembers that they move, slowly circling while the rest of the structure remains stationary (or vice versa) and spends some time thinking about the time he first realised they moved.

When he arrived, there was a discolouration, a darker patch two metres across on one of the longways bands below one of the adjacent cubes. Although the inner surface of the structure is not entirely uniform, this was and has remained the only really noticeable feature he has seen. He called it Splodge.

Back then, he recalls, he used to bother to count the days, and then the months and years. Even when he forgot, he knew roughly where he was up to, and would start again from there. And then he lost his mind, for the first time. Despaired, tried to strangle himself, got really thin, that kind of thing. Mostly, he lay naked on his back all day, every day, and played with himself, swinging his penis left to right vacantly. When he eventually regained his sanity, he remembered that he had counted up to seventy years, or thereabouts. He didn't know how long he had been mad for, but that was a long time too.

A little while after recovering, he had noticed Splodge again. Waking up one day, he saw it right beneath his prism. In fact, it might have been Splodge which really brought him round; he couldn't now be sure.

Splodge had been good for him. He had come to think of it as a kind of dumb Man Friday, a native character, a friendly face in a foreign land. Eventually, as Splodge gradually moved slowly past, further and further away, he achieved a kind of peace, as if the little dark smudge had imparted a kind of wisdom to him, as a spirit guide might.

He isn't given to flights of fancy, and never anthropomorphised Splodge, but the relationship he developed with the stain was important, and the story it came to represent for him.

It is late, he has been remembering all evening. He sleeps through the night, but the light in his cube stays on. It took him many months to adjust to the constant light.

The man awakes in the morning, face down. The position he arrived in. His clothes have been removed, and are neatly folded in the position they were yesterday, the position they are always in.

The prism/prison doesn't make sense. It is always clean, pristine in fact, but he gets to keep his clothes, which are quite grubby at times. Every now and then, when he wakes up they feel cleaner, more or less in synchronisation with the routine he kept while aboard Tug 44.

He doesn't eat; he doesn't defecate, urinate, or sweat. His sexual desire is absent. He has been purified. Why, then, let him keep his clothes? Or why not clean them everyday? His teeth feel brushed intermittently, between two and three days, again the routine he would have kept before coming here. But his fingernails are restored every day, no matter how much he bites them, and his hair never grows. The elements which make up his constant maintenance are incongruous, and he thinks, not for the first time, that it would have been quicker for him to come to terms with if everything had made sense. Total stasis, nudity, an absolute sanitization.

Still, if he didn't have his clothes, he couldn't play sockball, and he supposes that it would have felt more like death to be so sterile.

Still lying face down on the floor, he thinks about the time he broke his leg. His knee, he thinks, actually. The memory is absolutely clear, but his physiological understanding isn't. 32nd sockball championships, qualifying round. A rebound over his head, and then some ridiculous lunging turn, a desperate manoeuvre, interrupted by a slip and a deafeningly loud crack. Followed by endless screaming.

He'd panicked, of course. 'That's the end of it.' He repeated, as he had said so at the time. An eternity twisted and bruised, further injuries to the back, shoulders and other leg as a result of hobbling around. Next day though, upon waking, you were fine, he muses.

Many memories have been lost to him, particularly from before his arrival. Those which remain, and the best of those from all the endless merged days inside, like the discovery of Splodge and his many serious sockball accidents, have crystallised into little points of time so clear that he feels he can physically reach inside his mind and pluck them out, unwrap them and look at the contents. As if, subconsciously, he has focused in on what is most precious and locked it, permanently un-changeable, so the endless years of life cannot strip them away, replace all his memories with identical visions of his current state. He thinks that used to happen anyway, the freezing of important memories to protect them into the onset of old age, but not to this extent.

To him, these memories are like watching a film, in super super high definition, played back to him crisp and clean. Or better still, acted out for him in real life.

I bet no-one else has experienced that kind of memory. I'm the only one, he thinks.

He plucks another from its nook and opens it up.

He remembers the time when it became very cold, the start of a very bad time for him. A few years, he remembers, where he slept in his clothes and still shivered, developed his second madness. He got angry, and shouted a lot, railing against the forces which had stolen his life from him, such as it was. Splodge was still around then, had only just crept below the next cube, but he was only really starting to get to grips with the lessons he would take away from those times. He wasn't prepared.

He doesn't know what caused the cold, but he has had fun imagining. A popular morning thought, in fact. An area of space filled with icy gas? Or, if on a planet, a short ice age? Or a malfunction of course. Boring.

Of course, at the time, the fact that the cold had just stopped didn't bring him round. He was bitter for many years, and planned his terrible vengeance against whoever had created this ring. Being immortal, or so he thought, he imagined he could harness this power somehow to smash his way free, and would occasionally launch himself at the walls of his living space with reckless abandon, breaking fingers and arms and once, cracking his skull.

He chuckles, as an older brother might amuse himself by watching the ill advised antics of a small sibling. The laugh pushes his torso up from the floor, and jiggles him around a bit, which makes him laugh even more.

Life in the prism is not too bad for him, you see. After navigating certain mental barriers, the most important being a belief he was not imprisoned, but castaway, hence the importance of Splodge in its capacity as Man Friday.

A castaway. A man experiencing a change of circumstances, rather than containment intended by another, and the old adage that one man's island paradise is another man's desolate wasteland.

Three tricks of the mind assist with this.

Number one, he begins. I was never free. I was always trapped to a degree, though the space I was trapped in was generally larger. He repeats the catechism in his head.

Number two. I am not being watched, there is no purpose to my situation and no reason for it. He repeats the catechism in his head, and dwells on its meaning. I first thought that I was watched in the Tug, that little cabin smaller than my prism, and that this was planned, but now I believe that something automatic brought me here. Something automatic that has no further interest in me, could not have interest in anything. Something that should have been switched off but wasn't, or something which broke down.

Number three. I am not wasting my life. He repeats the catechism in his head, and explores it. I used to perform a boring job, repetitive, monotonous, piloting a grimy little ship, ostensibly to keep larger ships out of trouble they never got into. Sitting and sweating in a cramped cockpit 12 hours a day, months on end, for a half decent wage but terrible pension and benefits. I was going to die, eventually, maybe after a few brief years of lukewarm retirement. Or maybe die in the cockpit, facedown amongst the food wrappers and magazines. That was wasting my life. Now I'm trapped in a boring, repetitive routine not of my choosing, but I haven't died, and I haven't aged. I could only waste something which is finite, and I haven't got anything of that nature.

I'm a castaway, living in safety and comfort, unable to take part in all of the vain pursuits of life, that in all probability are obsolete by now.

These days, he feels a sense of contentment he never had in his old life, and he's quite happy to live forever. Things are just about to get interesting again, anyway, he thinks, from his prone attitude on the floor. Today is the 51st sockball finals. And on the lateral bands forming the inside edge of the cavern, way out on the boundary beyond which clear visual details are lost, he thinks he's just spotted an old friend returning.

Kate Brown

Kate Brown's films *Julie and Herman* and *Absolutely Positive* have been shown on television and at film festivals worldwide. She studied film directing at the National Film and Television School. Her short fiction has been published in various online magazines, broadcast on Radio Netherlands and is forthcoming with Cinnamon Press. She's been short-listed for the Fish Short Story Prize, the Fish One Page Prize and the Asham Award. Kate has almost finished her first novel. After living in Amsterdam for the last ten years, this summer Kate is moving to Berlin. She blogs at www.katebrown.nl.

Two Girls Under an Apple Tree

That was the moment I knew my sister had been possessed by the devil; when she reached her long slim arm up between the boughs of the tree and picked the plump, blushing apple. I gazed at the strand of auburn hair that had escaped her black fur trimmed cap; a glowing will-o'-the-wisp, an ember from the fire. I looked down at the neatly manicured lawn, at my sister's new black shoes, her tight black stockings. My own cap was white; my clogs, too.

She held the apple out to me.

I shook my head.

My sister smiled. 'That's not like you.'

I didn't tell anyone the devil had taken my sister. Instead, when father led us in prayer before we ate our evening meal, I tried to pray twice as hard as before. Praying harder threw each word around my head, thumping inside my temples. It hurt. My sister smiled and passed me the bread. She had a sweet smile, I could see why the devil wanted her. But I wanted to save her from him. I wanted him to give her back.

My mother helped me with things like grazed knees and torn skirts. She also taught me some valuable lessons: how to pick up stones the village children threw at me and hurl them back again, how to keep going when the mad woman who lived on the other side of the stream cursed me for trying to cross the trickle of water she considered hers. I did not think my mother would be a match for the devil. She was too kind, and sometimes I could trick her if I had done something wrong and didn't want her to know: like the day I fell in the stream and soiled my newest dress, but told her the mad woman had pushed me.

That my father could drive the devil away, I did not doubt. When I was very small, our stable boy had forgotten to secure the girth of father's saddle properly. Father had fallen from his horse, breaking his arm. With the broken arm hanging limp at his side, he beat the boy so severely he could not walk for a week.

Until the day she picked the apple, I hadn't realised how much time my sister spent under that tree. How she sheltered hungrily in the dappled shadows.

'I want my skin to stay milky white,' she told me, when I asked her what she was doing there. 'I don't want to be like Anneke.'

Anneke was our neighbour. She worked in her father's fields from dawn to dusk.

'I like Anneke,' I said.

'So do I. I just don't want her skin.'

We were wealthy. My sister could afford to sit under the apple tree. Sometimes she took a book with her when our father was out.

'I want to learn,' she said.

Knowledge was bad for you. I knew that, for my sister hid her book when she saw our father coming home. My mother indulged her with a silent smile. I wondered whether she too had read books under trees when she was a young woman.

The only book we were supposed to read was the Bible. My sister wouldn't let me see what the book was that she was reading, but I knew it was not Our Lord's. It was too slim a volume and our bible was bound in a deep purpley red. This book was blue.

Keeping her skin milky white was just one of the reasons my sister lingered under the apple tree. The tree was near our garden gate. If you opened the gate and stepped outside, you were in the World. I was allowed to climb on the gate and talk to the neighbours as they passed by, as long as I promised not to swing on its wrought iron curls. A year ago, my sister had been allowed to play there with me, but since her breasts had started growing, the reins restricting her had grown tighter.

Pieter, a boy from the village passed by once a day. My sister would leave her place under the apple tree, go over to our evergreen hedge and pretend to pick flowers from it, even though there were none. I think it was Pieter who slipped her the book.

The day I saw my sister kissing Pieter I was at my perch on the garden gate, watching two swallows chase each other in near perfect circles. I hadn't seen my sister leave the garden, she must have gone out when I was in the kitchen helping mother, stringing beans.

'Freija!' I shouted.

My sister ignored me and elbowed her way into the garden, almost knocking me off the gate. I wanted to tell her about the swallows. I wanted to ask her what it was like to kiss a boy. But her mind was on other things; things more important than me.

I could smell the summer honeysuckle as I knocked on my father's study door. It was the only door in the house that did not stand open on such a warm evening. As he called for me to enter, I heard my sister shout gaily to my mother outside. They were tending my mother's herb garden. I couldn't hear what my sister said, but I could tell that she was happy.

Freija screamed far louder than the stable boy. My father said it meant that the devil was buried deep within her. That we had only just got there in time. On her second scream, I hid my head under the bedclothes. My tears all came at once in a hot gush. Struggling further beneath the covers, tunnelling myself to a place where I would not hear, the feather eiderdown almost suffocated me. That was what I wanted. To never have to come out. After beating her, my father locked my sister in the cellar. Downstairs, I could hear my mother crying, too. Then I heard a slap.

The next day, a small swarm of bees gathered near the garden gate. I went close, I circled them. I wanted them to sting me, but the bees followed Pieter when he passed by. I didn't have a chance to tell him what had happened.

I went into the house. I wanted my mother. I wanted to string beans again. As I made my way into the kitchen, my clogs struck against the worn flagstones in the scullery. Apart from the sound of my shoes, it was silent. My mother wasn't there. She had said nothing since the slap, keeping away from father. And from me. Through the kitchen window, I could see her in the bit of garden behind the house, bent studiously over her herbs; I couldn't see her face, but I could guess her expression was grim. I went back outside. I swung on the gate, hoping someone would notice and scold me.

That evening, my mother took bread and water down to the cellar, I listened to her each and every step. My sister did not eat. Not that day, nor the next. Even my father began to show signs of worry; wringing his big hands together as he prayed about some abstraction or other, even he could not quite pretend.

At the edge of the lawn nearest to the house was a patch of grass that had been neglected enough for some daisies to sprout. If I sat among the flowers I had a view of the metal grille that let air into the cellar. Air, the one and only thing keeping my sister alive, apart from a few sips of water. She was drinking a little, mother said, but not enough. How much longer would my sister stay alive if she did not eat?

I watched as my father got on his horse (he had saddled it himself since the incident of the broken arm) and rode towards the village. He looked proud. I hated him for what he had done, but I hated myself more. When Pieter walked by that morning, he glanced nervously at the house and quickened his step. Mother had warned him. As I watched him go, I beheaded daisies, ripping their fragile flowers from the milky, bleeding stems. A summer storm was brewing. Dark clouds collected and an erratic wind began to ruffle the leaves on the apple tree. I got up, went over, and stood as still as I could underneath it, listening. The boughs creaked gently; a friendly sound. I looked up between its branches.

I dug the milking stool out from under a pile of hay in the stable. It had not been thrown away after my grandmother died. She had kept cows. She had believed in keeping cows, my mother said, even though she was not particularly good at it. It had been a kind of faith.

I went back to the apple tree. I stood on the stool and reached a short chubby arm up through its branches.

My sister's fur trimmed cap was the first thing I saw when I peered through the grille. She was sitting hunched up, facing away from me, into the darkest corner of the room. I thrust my arm down between the bars of the grille and held the apple out towards her.

'Freija,' I whispered. I saw her back tense, but she did not turn around.

I called a little louder.

'Freija. Please.'

Darci Bysouth

Darci Bysouth was born and raised in the ranch lands of Western Canada, but has made Edinburgh her home for the last fifteen years. She teaches reading and writing to primary school children who experience difficulties, and finds their creative and unique ways of looking at the world a constant source of inspiration. She has studied creative writing and writing for screen through evening classes, and has just finished writing her first novel.

Marrakech

'Marrakech,' my mother would say, 'Marrakech was somewhere else.'

She'd peel off my rain-dampened tights and drape them over the back of a chair in front of the coal fire. They'd steam silently, and everything I hated about my childhood was there in that fusty odour of wool.

'In Marrakech, the sun beat down hot and the air smelled medieval,' my mother would say as I stretched out my legs, watching the red chafe rise. 'Oh God, the perfumes of the medina! Cumin and coriander, and attar of roses. Cinnamon sticks and seed pods of cardamom, the turmeric a dry shocking gold. The souk stall vendors would pile them up in pyramids of colour, and their little burners blazed day and night with benzoin. Did you know that the old plague doctors, they'd strap beaks of posies to their noses, to drive away the smells of sickness? Little pouches of aromatics to hang round their necks, that too. Those spices, they clear the stench of the dead unburied, they carry off every bad memory on a drift of petal.'

Her eyes would stray then, they'd dart over the clash of scarves floated over the second hand sofa and the intricately patterned rugs that hid the worst of the scratched floorboards. The mention of Marrakech often made her restless. She'd spring up to open a window despite the cold outside and her hands would flutter and float until they found her basket of yarns.

'The rugs so well woven,' she'd say, her hands calming over the clacking needles, 'Perfectly patterned, balanced and geometric. No people, you know, nothing real allowed in those rugs.'

Our home was filled with her knitting. She had her own sense of colour, my mother, with shades grouped according to semantics rather than aesthetic compatibility. Saffron needed its fiery nature calmed with imperial purple, the wildness of lime required taming by sludge brown, and all these hues worked out their issues on our living room cushions. My mother painted my bedroom walls sky blue and knitted my bedspread shades of orange. She would have me sleep with the setting sun. Every night, she'd wrench open a window and instruct the whistling wind to blow the bad dreams away and keep me safe.

We lived in one of the little flats favoured by students, although my mother had never been to university. I was sometimes invited to a classmate's birthday party or Saturday sleepover. Other children lived in whole houses and their living rooms were carpeted in pale modern shades with black lamps and hard-edged ornaments in red. Their mothers came home from work with their hair pinned up over big-shouldered suits and their lips glossed crimson. They'd smile tiredly and kick off pointy pumps to rub their toes, telling us to eat our crisps at the kitchen table. All those shiny surfaces showed fingerprints.

Our flat was not shiny. It was frequently hazy with smoke from the cigarettes my mum smoked constantly, or from the incense she lit to hide the smell. My mother wore squat sandals with woolly socks and kept her shoes on in the house. I'd ask why she did not wear smart suits like the other mothers, or go out to work in high heeled pumps. I kept my eyes wide and my voice pleasant, but I knew what I was doing. My mother's hands would flutter and reach for another cigarette, and my guts would twist.

'Marrakech,' she'd muse, 'In Marrakech we all wore little slippers and shuffled the streets, slow in the heat of the sun. Little slippers, some of them satin and embroidered with flowers, some of them fastened with silver bells. Like harem girls, we were, padding soft and silent around the sleeping sultan.'

I had sturdy soled sandals bought in the second hand shops. The gym teacher would not let me take PE lessons without trainers, and sent increasingly strident letters home advising my mother of the school rules. My mother would fold and tear these notes, skewering the quarters to the nail protruding from kitchen wall. They would join the reminders of appropriate school uniform, and the overdue library notices and electricity bills. I was instructed not to open the door should a man come knocking. I hid the notes my mother sent back to my teachers; I could not bear the brown butcher's paper they were written on.

I'd pick sly holes in my mother's knitting out of spite. My mother would say nothing while her hands unravelled the yarn to start over again. The local craft shop had agreed to take her work, and the jumpers and scarves glared out their dissonances from the dim of the back corner. My mother would drag me there at the end of every month and sometimes the shop owner would smile and hand us an envelope of money. More often, we would leave with our arms piled high with the unsold merchandise, the gaudy colours amplifying my shame.

I would have to wear the worst of it. No point in spending money when we had perfectly good clothes in our hands, my mother would announce, and look at the spice market shades of this or the desert sun in that, surely this is the antidote to all the rain we've been having lately? My hatred would spike pure and hot, and blacker than any storm cloud.

I knew I would have to hurry cold and jumperless out the school gates, until the obscurity of hedges just before our flats. Quickly on over my head then, with the clashing hat pulled low over my face, just a short slink through the side street and I would be safely home.

Sometimes I would be caught out anyway, with the earthy shades of my packed lunch noticed or the lack of parent pointed out on open afternoon. I would come home drenched in drizzle and bristling with humiliation. My mother would peel off my rainbow colours and run me a bath.

'Did I tell you,' my mother would ask, her hands aflutter, 'Did I tell you about the Hammam, the public baths?'

'Picture us then, a line of women making our way there in the afternoon. We'd enter the steamy room one by one to wait our turn; we'd stand there naked in all our ages but unashamed. This was another country, you know, and the usual rules of propriety did not apply. They'd float petals in the water for us and the smell of roses and jasmine made my head drift. The bravest went first into that scalding hot water and the weakest waited until it had become tepid and cloudy. They'd scrub us down with rough loofahs, and they were not gentle with it, but how clean you were after! How floaty free you felt! Darling, you will take the Hammam with me some day.'

I'd ask about the men, my eyes averted.

'The men? Ah the men, we never saw them, they went to the baths in the morning.'

Sometimes I would wonder aloud about my father, about why there was no father in my house. I was crafty; I'd let the question drift out like an afterthought. My mother would change the subject. She would tell me about Marrakech.

'Did I tell you,' she'd say, 'Did I tell you that I had an admirer there?'

She met him at the medina. His dark eyes followed her as she wandered, as she pointed and mimed at the exotic fruits, as she laughed when they did not understand her garbled attempts at their dialect. The men brushed past, sometimes lingering a little too long and a little too close. One of them smiled and made reassuring sounds while he tried to force her into a back room. Her admirer rescued her, and he became both her interpreter and her protector.

'We'd take mint tea in the cafe.' my mother smiled, 'He'd ask me question after question in that odd English of his, his hands stilled and waiting. His dark eyes would never leave mine when I spoke. I had his undivided attention and sometimes I fear it went to my head, for I would tell him the most fantastic stories. He would ponder whatever I said with the same sobriety. He had a bald head and he was not young but it didn't matter, he was by far the best listener I had ever known. Soon I was in love with him.'

'What happened next?' I'd ask grudgingly, taken in again.

'Ah well,' sighed my mother, 'Good listeners are few and far between, and that quality is particularly rare in a man. I had a rival; another western lady much like myself but blonder and with eyes a deeper shade of blue. She connived and lied, she worked her manipulations and soon my lover and myself were separated. I saw him sometimes, sometime after, but his hands would not rest. They played with his spoon, they stirred the sugar into his tea, and round and round they went. I talked, and his eyes strayed from mine to his hands to the little whirlpool they made. I could not abide the smell of mint after, you know.'

She could tell a story, could my mother. I would almost forgive her the gauzy skirts and circus colours, the frizzed and hennaed hair clown-like and comic. I could almost forget the atrocities of my hand-knitted childhood. Then the kids at school would see her at the shops with me in tow. They'd giggle and mime the smoking of a joint, with glassy eyed gaze and benevolent smile.

'Hippie,' they'd snigger, 'Hey man, where'd I leave my hash?'

My mother never touched drugs that I knew, not even painkillers or penicillin. She distrusted doctors and modern medicine. I would be given salt water gargles and teaspoons of honey when I had a cold, I would have rose water compresses for a rash. I snuck out to the parties in those clean modern houses some years later and I was passed acrid smelling pipes and little neon patches of paper. I saw the eyes slanted sideways at each other, then at me, and I knew myself unsafe. I worked hard at school instead and I got a scholarship to the university.

I studied sociology and I knew we were disadvantaged, I studied history and I knew we were the remnants of a counter culture. I studied cynicism and I understood that the difference between rich hippies and the real ones was the cut of their clothes and the duration of their delusions. I came home for the holidays and I talked to my mother.

'What happened?' I asked, 'between Marrakech and this. What happened?'

'Oh darling,' she said, 'Life. Life happened.'

She was working part time in a new age shop then. She dressed in all the colours of her aura and told the customers about crystals. Her hand-knit things still lurked in the back, and sometimes they sold for prices that almost justified their cacophony. The nineties had arrived with their promise of gentler times, and our way of life was nearly mainstream by then. The university students did yoga and hung tie dyed scarves on their walls, they'd rediscovered patchouli and mismatched woollens, and suddenly it was hip to recycle paper. My mother got a discount on sticks of sandalwood and she was happy.

I studied economics and I knew we were insignificant. My mother had drifted free of the system; she had made little contribution to labour, she neither banked nor borrowed, and she had neither savings nor pension. She had drifted free and she was not safe.

I went to work in a bank. I bought a pair of glossy red pumps with my first paycheque and took out an investment portfolio with my second. A percentage of my earnings appeared on the cheque I sent my mother every month. I bought a glossy red car to go with the pumps and I was happy. I worked hard, I spent money, I aspired to the same things as everyone else. I bought a flat and furnished it in neutral shades with accents of red and I was safe.

I attracted my own admirers. I would reheat things from the better shops in my gleaming chrome kitchen and, after a glass or two of deep red wine, I would tell stories about my mother. Her ghastly colours and the hand-knitted horrors, her insistence on an open window despite the weather. I was good with the descriptions and my admirer would gaze at me, rapt. The punchline was always Marrakech and he'd laugh accordingly. I could smile too, I could afford to be a bit of a character now that I was safe.

If my guts twinged, if I remembered how my mother's hands could flutter when I hurt her, I reminded myself of that monthly payment. I still talked to mother, I phoned every month and she told me about the colours she had knit into her newest project, or how the man with the bad stomach had benefited from the application of tourmaline. I would listen, I would tell her I was glad she was keeping busy while flipping through my accounts.

She began to talk about Marrakech again, about how she would go back one day. I didn't hear any change in her voice. I could not hear the cells mutating and multiplying but I think she could.

The call came late one Tuesday, and I arranged a week off work. The hospital stank the way hospitals do, with the sickly sweet odour of urine layered between bleach and some kind of floral disinfectant. My mother lay with bright hair frizzed round her, like a pale-stemmed rose between neutral sheets.

The doctors said it was advanced, there would be little time.

'These doctors, you know I never liked them much,' said my mother from between parched lips. I pressed for more, I hated that these might be her last words.

'Marrakech,' I said, 'Tell me about the medina, the souk. Tell me about your admirer.'

'Marrakech,' said my mother, 'It was somewhere else. It smelled of cinnamon and roses, of benzoin burning.'

I had her cremated, I knew how she hated to be shut in.

There were many things to sort after; my mother had kept things over the years. I found a bundle of unopened letters in her dresser drawer.

My aunt was willing to meet with me. She sits across from me at my kitchen table now and her eyes are very blue. She smokes and I say nothing, I can smell something of my mother in that dusty sweet odour.

'Ah, your mother,' she says, 'She was always an odd one. Off in her own world, you know? The stories she told! Like a film, they were, all the colours and smells there and told so clear. She might have made movies or written books if it weren't for the breakdown. Different days, them, you acted strange and you were noticed, you were taken away.'

'Your mother spent time in hospital,' my aunt says, 'Mental hospital, I mean. Went to visit her and I was appalled. Stink of the place, that got you first, then that sickly pale green everywhere. Her doctor was a pure creep. Sucked on breath mints and stared at you.

Baldy wee bastard. Heard he was done for having it off with the patients.'

51

'Now the last straw,' my aunt says, 'that was the baths. Like something medieval, it was. They lined up all the women naked as the day they was born, no dignity there, and made them wait their turn. They ran the water so hot that the first in would be scalded, they scrubbed so hard they drew blood. I saw that and I knew I had to get your mother out.'

'I argued, I lied, I sweet-talked that baldy doctor and finally I threatened. He caved in, he knew I had his number.' My auntie exhales and it sounds like a sigh.

'Your mother never forgave me. I think she was sweet on the creep, he'd done some of that mind control on her, you know? They had hotels for mental patients just out of hospital back then and your mother lived in one for a while. Run by hippies. She had to leave after she had you, they didn't allow kids, and that's the last I knew. I wrote at Christmas, I sent a card on your birthday and hers, but she never wrote back.'

My auntie stubs out her cigarette and looks at me. Her eyes are a bluer version of my mother's, and her hair might have been blonde once. I don't ask about Marrakech. I can guess how her eyes will cloud in confusion and how her mouth will form the denial.

I will open the window once she leaves, then I will sit down at my computer. A flight will be easy enough to find, it is a popular holiday destination amongst those looking to escape the winter rain. I will not take my red pumps or my grey suits, this is another country and the usual rules of propriety will not apply. I'll buy the gauziest of skirts at the souk, I'll clash my colours freely and shuffle the streets in squat sandals.

I'll go with my mother of course. I think of her carried like a little pouch of aromatics around the neck, and I smile, I think she will forgive me the aesthetics for the semantics. We will wallow in the perfumes of the medina and our memories will unravel like bad knitting. We will drench ourselves in the rainbow colours of the souk and be safe from the darker realities. We will take the Hammam and we will float free as rose petals scattered. I'll go with my mother and we will be somewhere else together.

Joanna Campbell

Joanna Campbell is forty-nine and has three beautiful daughters. She once had shoulder pads, big hair and worked in retail and finance. She was very bad at it. She is now supposed to be her husband's secretary, but is dreadful at that too. She loves writing. It absorbs every hour she should spend filing or dusting. She has had several stories published in *Writers' Forum* and various women's magazines, including *The Yellow Room*. The fund-raising book, *100 Stories For Haiti*, includes one by Joanna.

Struthio Camelus

Walking to the interviewer's desk, I lose all the sight in my right eye and a section in the left. I slip a little. Fortunately, I have already absorbed the layout of the office. This is a confidence-boosting ploy from the book *Face Yourself*.

If you let your eyes sweep for six seconds across an intimidating space, such as an exam hall or indeed an interview room, you feel at home. Not in the way that might induce slumping or scratching at your armpit, but in a way that melts you into your surroundings. So I've absorbed the cheese plant sulking in the corner, the thin brown carpet tiles and even the nibbled polystyrene ceiling tiles.

Then you follow your nose. Smell your new air. Breathe hard through your nostrils and fill them with lilies or coffee or fresh emulsion or, in my case, a damp St Bernard. My eyes mist before I see him. Of course my nose doesn't specify the breed, but knows it's moist dog hair. And Mr Groves is telling me that the beast is called Courvoisier and that his barrel is sadly empty. So I make my deductions.

My ears are keen. They pick up ice chinking in Mr Grove's glass, a humming fridge and laboured breathing. The latter could be Mr Groves, Courvoisier or me. Or all of us. There! That's what the book wants you to achieve. Unification. Harmony with your new space and all who exist within it. Easy.

In this way, you can glide to your seat and emit natural charm. Of course my stumble jars the entrance I imagined making, but I reach the seat, steady myself and thrust out my hand for a manly shake, one second before my left leg gives way.

Now Mr Groves may think I'm sitting down a shade too soon and far too suddenly, but he's an old-fashioned mannerly gent with a rich fruitcake voice, very English. He may like eccentrics. His under manager, Mr Hennessy, isn't in the room. Shame. He splutters, my research tells me, and his seventeen stone frame oozes lazily over his chair. Easy to impress his type when you're a young thruster. *Play to your strengths*, the book says.

The book also advises composed posture, so as not to appear desperate. However, it doesn't say how to do this when you become blind and your leg crumples.

But I'm doing well. I know the plant and the carpet. And the piles of newspapers littering his desk. I have my collection of smells and sounds. Mr Groves is talking and I incline my head to demonstrate my listening powers. I hope I'm training my eyes on his face, but I might be staring at the hat stand I'd spotted behind him on the right. So I move my head a little left, just in case. It's always best to pay attention to detail.

'So, Mr Daniel, I notice that your application form shows gaps in your employment history. I would be most obliged if you could fill those in for me. Tell me, for example, what you did in the missing six months after you left the ostrich farm.'

I can tell he's smiling encouragement. It's throbbing in his plummy voice. I'm sure he's leaning forward on the desk, arms on his blotter and fingers spread to invite candour. He doesn't want me to hide anything.

Well, I've read the book, so I know better than to conceal the truth. *Show your cards*, I read only last night, and then you won't be guilty of cheating others or yourself.

I think back. In those missing months, I was with Emily.

We climbed a small mountain in Wales and became slowly stupefied by the wine we drank on the summit. It led us into a pact. We planned to spend a long time climbing other mountains and earning no money. I had nothing to lose, because I was already bankrupt and drank a lot. Emily had a good flat in Cardiff and an open mind. She agreed before our bottle finally emptied that she would sell up and fund the trip.

We didn't like calling it a trip. It was more of a tangent. A deviation. A potential transformation.

She was having doubts on the way down, I could tell. I'm astute with women. When they fall silent, if they purse their lips and look away, but upwards, then it's a proper sulk. If they look down with their teeth biting on their lower lip, then they're worried. Emily was worried.

I promised we would get married afterwards. I knew that would clinch it. She was a soft and pillowy girl, who cooed at babies. She had been cast adrift by several ships panting in the night, when I sailed into her life. Actually, she came to the shop at the farm to buy an ostrich steak for her Dad's birthday and I wooed her from the meat counter with my bloodied apron on.

I had absolutely no intention of marrying Emily of course. But pretending isn't the same as lying. We all pretend, but we aren't all liars, are we? There were other girls with perfect undulations, other hills to conquer, and I would not have liked to erase them from my future. The book says that you only have the future. Nothing else. When you think about it, it's true. Without a future, what is there?

But I gave Emily the perfect picture, all misty and gilt-edged, with white dresses and orange blossoms, and she came off that mountain in Wales, sold her flat and gave me the money.

When I left her warm and beatific in bed to gallantly buy the tickets and climbing gear, I hopped on a train to Switzerland and ate chocolate in a wooden chalet for six months. It's liberating to act on a whim.

Swiss money soon runs out and I decided that I would start again in an English office, far from Wales. I want to shuffle paper and pen-push. Slam filing cabinets shut and answer telephones with 'Daniel speaking.' Have a metal nameplate in front of me – Mr Daniel, Loan Advisor. At heart, I want to be a dependable chap. I want to be trusted with the combination of the safe. Do the daily banking...

'Mr Groves, I'll be honest, I was in a Swiss sanatorium. My lungs were diseased. I recovered only after a prolonged fight. Twice they thought they'd lost me.' I cough gently and feel Groves moving closer to me, smell his breakfast kipper.

'Twice I saw a pure light guiding me out of my suffering. I faced it, faced the truth of my impending death, touched the robes of angels. But, Mr Groves, I wasn't ready. There is more for me to do. I want to serve the public. I want to help them buy the roof over their heads, allowing newly-weds to have babies, giving shelter to families weathering the daily storms of life. I want to work all week, just Sunday free, for church. I live in a modest boarding house. That's all I need for my own personal happiness.'

Research is the key, the book says. I know Groves is deeply religious. I wish I'd known about drooling St Bernards though. I wouldn't have worn my better pair of shoes.

I feel the sensation vanish in my other leg as Groves is phrasing his next question. My arm is tingling too and my face feels full of pins and needles. When I fold my hands together, hot lumps emerge, which begin to itch. I try sitting on them, but Groves is saying, 'Ah, here's a cup of tea for you, Mr Daniel. I always have tea at eleven.'

Silly old duffer. How can I take the cup with my hands in flames? Where will I put it on the cluttered desk? With my sight so bad, I'll spill it for sure.

Using the tiny strip of vision remaining in my left eye, I take the saucer gingerly and hear the cup slither. I have to bend to it and slurp. There's nothing else I can do. I'm in such pain I can't poke my finger through the handle properly. I feel the steam rise into my eyes, but there's no scalding on my tongue. It's numb. It's enormous in my mouth. The tea runs off my lips and onto my trousers. I lean close to the desk, almost ramming the edge of it into my eye and set the capering cup down on the stack of papers. The old fool ought to have the Financial Times, but all I can discern are locals from the length and breadth of England. Echoes, Heralds, News & Journals, Advertisers and Daily Presses.

'Are you quite all right down there, Mr Daniel?'

'Oh, yes, perfectly fine. Indeed.'

Daft beggar. There's a big ornate key on top of the pile. I tingle at the thought of inserting it into the safe. When I walked in, I saw the hulking grey beauty, beckoning me like an overblown mistress, in the other corner from the cheese plant. I can smell her metallic scent, almost feel her smooth, cool flanks...

But I must concentrate. *Make yourself seem indispensable*, the book says. Easy as a hot knife through butter.

'For example, Mr Daniel, how would you, if offered the job, help me to steal?'

My stomach lurches and my ears feel hot. What? How does the book expect me to answer this? Oh yes, I know! *Trick Questions and Surprises!* This idiot is so predictable.

'Very good, Sir, I like your sense of humour!'

Always butter them up. They love it.

'But I mean it, Mr Daniel. I want to poach business from the floundering branches in the northern region, who are losing their mortgage-seeking clientele. My trusty locals tell me about their house prices.' He patted his papers. 'Stuffy little managers who stick to the regulations about lending money. Not a clue how to doctor the applicant's payslip, increase their income on paper, sweet-talk HQ into fast-forwarding the paperwork before the auditors interfere. You see, the more we lend, the more we make. And then what happens, Mr Daniel?'

'Er...'

'We get Branch Of The Year of course! A dinner at the big Italian in the High Street and a trophy for the staff room. And a tie for me. Oh, and the branch ascends one or two notches in the ranking. We'd be a Grade Three. That allows us to hold more cash on the premises. I love a well-stocked safe. Easy money, eh, Mr Daniel?'

The floor is moving under my feet. My head is full of manic fish flicking their tails, swimming round and round. This clown is getting under my skin. He's turning Chapter Ten on its head: *Always Stay On Top In The Conversation*. I'm trapped in this room, being ripped to shreds, piece by piece. The harmony's gone.

He seemed so harmless at first. Avuncular and doddery. My research tells me he likes general knowledge quizzes and any local papers. He just spends his life sucking up and spouting out facts. Big, small, national, international, mundane or incredible. If it's a fact or a snippet or a nugget of information, he sponges it up. He wears a knitted waistcoat, for God's sake. I thought he'd eat out of my hand.

'Did the ostriches eat out of your hand, Mr Daniel?'

I might faint. He can read my mind. I'm in so many pieces, it's probably hanging out of my head.

'I ask about these creatures, Mr Daniel, because I need prizes for my raffle. The manager that sells the most tickets gets a free holiday. I read about an ostrich farm in the Midlands.' He patted his pile of papers. 'I see their leather makes bags and purses. Highly desirable luxuries with a quill pattern. If you were to return there and procure a few for me, I would draw a veil over your, er, little indiscretion, shall we call it?' He taps the papers with the colossal safe key. I hear it thudding up and down on the South Wales Post.

I know the headline. He'll Be Conning Up The Mountain or some such. I know the picture of me with an arm round the hapless Emily. I know when I'm in a tight corner. The book says that the only way to deal with a tight corner is *Distraction*. Do something drastic to divert the attention of the person ensnaring you. Groves has to believe he's got the wrong man, that I'm not the conman in the paper. After all, I've changed my name a few times. I was Craig Carstairs then.

I never forget a face, Mr Daniel. Or should I say, Mr Carstairs?

Courvoisier is growling by my ankle. Time for the drastic action. But it happens anyway. No input from me at all.

My body throws itself on the carpet, writhing like a snake with colic. The dog places a paw on my stomach and drools. My ears buzz, drowning out all other sound and coherent thought. I want to shout for Groves to call 999, but I have no power of speech left. I would give anything to feel the touch of his hand. Even the dog is some comfort.

Then I hear him, very close to my ear, as though he is speaking through grit.

'Mr Daniel, you underestimate. That is where you are going wrong. Never kid a kidder. Didn't your textbook tell you that? Dear me, that is the very first rule. Followed by the importance of being truthful to yourself. Even if you lie through your teeth to everyone else. You have been denying your symptoms, have you not? Denial, Daniel, is bad, very bad.' Groves clicked his tongue a few times.

'Been burying your head in the sand, Daniel? Criminal, that is. Unless that's your stock-in-trade, of course.... In which case, you might just be forgiven. Your plumage is remarkable, I must say. Those silky black feathers you're sprouting would fetch quite a price. Then there's your leather. And the meat! I must say, it is delicious.'

I can feel my quills bursting forth.

'Bright cherry-red in the raw and like lean beef when roasted. Very low fat too.'

I'm quivering.

'Oh, you could end up a nine-footer, I believe. You grow that tall, I understand. Those long legs are good for running fast. Up to forty-five miles an hour. I could ride you. You're good at taking people for a ride, Daniel, aren't you?'

My legs are stretching. My feet burst out of their brogues. I have two repulsive toes per foot. With scaly skin.

'Two toes are good for sprinting. Better than four.'

My neck elongates painfully. I wriggle and kick out.

'I'll stand behind you I think, Daniel. You can only kick forwards.'

I lay my head and neck flat on the ground.

'Ah, yes I know about this too! Makes you look like a mound of earth from a distance. An unremarkable lump. Protects you from predators. Artful bugger, aren't you? Makes a change for you to be the one in fear, don't you think?'

I stay in position.

'And I believe your orange neck distinguishes you as one of the Masai variety. Quite attractive. If I send you back to the farm, I shall get a blooming good price for you. They'd make quite a few handbags out of you. Of course I kept Courvoisier as a companion, rather than send him to the kennels. Call me sentimental, but I just couldn't bear to part with him, slobbery old beast that he is.' I recall the missing Mr Hennessy.

'You might like to think you lay the largest eggs, but they are actually the smallest in relation to your size, young man. You're all feathers and legs, really. Not much use until you're on the butcher's slab.'

Ostriches have the largest eyes of all vertebrates on the land, he tells me.

I see everything clearly now. But my long legs are still a little shaky. I must think about this. I shake my rustling feathers to fluff them up. What does the book say about unexpected twists and turns? How do I return to harmony with my surroundings now? Where is my future?

I burrow my head up to my neck in the cheese plant pot.

Tara Conklin

Tara Conklin worked for many years as a lawyer in New York and London but is currently at home caring for her two young children and pursuing her life-long passion for writing fiction. She now lives in Seattle, Washington and is at work on a novel. This is her first published story.

Signs of Our Redemption

Freedom is a curious thing. Are the chickens free, running their fool heads off in the yard? Is the horse free, galloping in the pen and tossing its mane to scare off the flies? It still got to put on the harness, reins slip round its neck and that piece of iron tween its teeth. Mister say you only ever ride a horse hard when there's nothing else to be done or else next time he won't ride for you at all. Lottie tell me not to think on things like this. She say it'll end in no good, and that ain't no place to be. Sometimes I think Lottie my only friend in all the world, and if I listen to her right and tie my apron strings and bend my head to whatever task afore my eyes, then my heart will rest easy and calm.

Mister and his Pa built the big house out of wide yew beams and nails thick as your thumb. They painted it white, and the paint still there more or less, though peeling now in places round the door and near the upstairs windows where the moss's eaten its way in. The front door they built wide and tall, a proud front door, and the porch come out from the house like a bottom lip stick out from a face. Mister and Missus Lu sit out there on a summer night, rocking in the big rockers Missus Lu had old Winton make for her, and I hear the sound of their rocking, just a little creak creak, regular as rain. Most days I don't think of this house as a prison, but that's what it is all the same.

Missus Lu ask me yesterday if I'd take her to town, just us two. It's always Mister who take her, sometimes with old Winton driving the coach. I never go. I just know the house here and the stream, and the old dirt road that lead over to the Stanmore's plantation house. That house there is big, big as a ship, rooms enough for everyone in the county to sleep it seems and dance too. They've a big room that Missus Lu said sometimes they clear away all the furnishings and roll up the rug and just use for dancing, with Mr Stanmore on the fiddle and his man Hal playing spoons. Missus Lu went just the once. She don't go down there much no more, don't go much a anywhere. Which is why she surprised me so with her cravin for town.

'Just you and me Josephine, we'll buy us some new hats. You need a new hat, keep the sun offa your face.' Her skin white as milk, smooth as a peach. She wear her hat all day long, sit in the shade, walk careful over the mud in the yard. She was on the porch then, in one a her rockers, creaking away. I'd just finished clearing away the breakfast things and come out to sweep.

'Missus, who'll drive the horses?' I stop my sweeping and the dust settle back down, I see it turning in the air.

'Why you and me of course. Whoever said a woman can't drive a horse? I've been holding the reins since I was six years old on my daddy's farm.'

I didn't ask her if Mister had word of her idea. She look so happy, her eyes gazing down the road towards town already, her shoulders straight like they straining against the horses and wind in her face as we set out to buy us some new hats. I didn't have the heart to say boo.

Missus Lu not been herself lately. Ever since, well, ever since the barn burned down? Or the old cow Maisie stopped giving milk? I can't remember when it started off. For awhile now Missus Lu's days been passing her by without a nod in hello or good-bye. She laugh sometimes, sitting on her own on the porch or in the sitting room, and she cry too for no reason at all. Lottie say it's cause she never had no children of her own. I remember Missus Lu used to go down to where the fieldhand children played, over by the tall oak with the roots that rise and twist away from the earth so there's places to hide underneath, cool and dark. She would go down there and sit on one a them roots and clap her hands with them, sing songs, play hidey seek. She don't do that no more. Now seems hard to believe was the same Missus Lu that sat down there singing Round the Rosy, the same one sitting here now on the porch, wanting to go to town but not a thought as to how rightly she might get there.

Lottie down in the flowerbeds, pulling out golden rod and lady slipper. Missus call them weeds so Lottie pull them up, fling them back cross her shoulder into a pile on the grass. Lottie stopped pulling when Missus ask about town, and look up at me as I come down the steps to find old Winton. Lottie raise her eyebrows just a touch and smile. 'Mornin, child,' she say to me. 'Have yourself a good ol mornin now.' She knows the trouble with Missus.

Winton got half-way towards getting things ready for town, hooking up the coach and harnessing Little and Big, Mister's two swaybacked mares, before Mister notice anything untoward happening. But then a horse whinnied, the wind shifted and Mister must've sniffed something in the air. He came striding up from the fields, poplar switch in one hand, yelling: 'What in God's good earth is happening here? Who is taking these horses into town?'

Missus Lu just sat, creaking back and forth. I'd already brought out her boots and her travelling wrap ready for the journey. She waved a fan in her face to cool from the heat starting to rise as the day pass from morning to noon. She didn't look at Mister, and poor Winton not sure which way to turn, he look at Mister, then at Missus Lu and stood his hands on the horse's back, not moving any which way. Then Missus Lu start to sing, a low sad song, making sounds like the wind on a winter's night blowing through all the open spaces in the attic roof, sounds that made me shiver when I was a child til I grew customed to them. A body can grow customed to anything if the mind tell it so, Lottie always say to me. But I don't believe that to be true.

I can't make out the words of Missus Lu's song, just the tune. She don't look at Mister and he just stood there down in the yard, dirt streaked cross his face shining with sweat, his eyes dark and cloudy.

'Josephine, are you looking after your Missus?' he asks me, looking up at the porch.

'Yes'm.' I'm standing beside Missus Lu's chair. 'Yes'm, I am.'

Mister look to his right and then to his left like he looking out for someone on their way to help him outta this mess, a farm with earth too rocky to plow, a barn full of old and dying animals, a wife not right in the head.

Mister look to the right and to the left and then step up on the porch and strike me cross the face. I hear the whistling of it in my ears and the smack of skin and suddenly I'm looking back over my shoulder, down to where the fields start and the few men Mister got left are working there. I see a bare back and a hoe raised, and another man staring back up at the house, leaning on a rake.

Missus Lu don't say a word, just go on singing her song and now I hear the words:

Over the mountain, and over the moor
Hungry and weary I wander forlorn
My father is dead, and my mother is poor
And she grieves for the days that will never return

Was this the moment? Was this the first time I knew I would go? No, I knew this was coming, sure as coolness follows a rain. One slap, then another, then a thousand more, or maybe one, or maybe two. Then one day, a day like any other, this day, the last.

Mister brought his hand down and step off the porch. 'Put those horses back in the barn,' he say to old Winton, 'Rub em down good, not right for them to be waiting out here in the heat of the day.' He don't say nothing to Missus Lu. It's planting time now and they all busy. He won't be back to the house til suppertime, after the sun set and too dark to work.

My cheek smart from Mister's palm and I taste blood in my mouth. I watch the back of him go on down to the fields and I don't touch my cheek though I want to. I don't say nothing to Missus Lu and she don't say nothing to me. Just her rocking and singing, creaking of the porch floor beneath the curve of the chair, and her voice soft as cornsilk, soft as a child's skin.

Lottie always say Missus Lu look to me like I a daughter of sorts, but I don't see it that way. I still just like the horse, the chicken, something to be fed and housed, to do what I been born and raised to do. Lottie say

Jesus know the truth. She look for signs of our redemption, signs like the two-headed frog they done found in the river last summer, or the night the sky filled with lights falling, and it be so bright that all us at the house and down by the cabins woke and stood on the front lawn, even Mister and Missus Lu, all us together side by side, eyes open to that burning sky. Lottie say these all markers along the way, promises Jesus be coming soon. She waiting for Him, she tell me. But who I waiting for?

The rest of the day pass, my cheek grows stiff like the board I use for the wash. A storm gathers in the hills, I can see it shift from grey to black but not a drop falls here, though don't we need it. Night comes and Missus says when I pull the covers to her chin, 'Josephine, watch the rain now,' as though it's pouring outside her window and not in some far off place. I nod as I do to everything she says, foolish or wise, wicked or kind. My mother is laid under a mound of earth beyond Mister's far fields, beside a sickly ash with leaves that's always yellow when they should be green. That's where my mother rests.

Mister comes back late from the fields. Upstairs I lay awake and hear the sounds of him eating the supper I laid out, then his feet on the stairs and knocks and creaks of him readying for bed. Then it's quiet for a long spell.

I pull back the blankets and put on my shoes. I know each board of this floor that Mister and his Pa laid, I know each wail and whine, each spot where the wood now growing soft and weak. I know this house like it my own body, every curve and wrinkle. Mine but never mine.

I make my slow way down these stairs, out the wide front door, the porch rockers silent now, still as the dead and gone.

There's a moon tonight, just enough to see by, a slice thin as my smallest finger and no more. The storm rages far off, I can feel it in the air, and I'm running away from those clouds though I cannot say what the sky might bring me later on. I run. The ache of my feet. The thunder of my heart.

Rik Gammack

Rik Gammack originally wanted to paint the covers for science fiction and fantasy novels. However, after graduating from Art College he became a computer programmer instead, and when not working is easily distracted from writing by walking, drawing and photography. Despite this, he has had one novel of erotica published and several short stories (both erotica and science fiction, sometimes combined!). He has also self-published one of his own works, a fantasy, and is currently working on another novel involving circuses, hot air balloons and licentious burlesque. His short story *Cheddar Gorging* won the *Cambridge Writers' Short Story Competition 2008*.

A Sense of Humour

Hey, let me tell you, dying ain't so bad. Piece of cake, really. At least, it is when you can afford a Resurrection policy, which – apart from a mountain of money – involves nothing more onerous than having your mind regularly scanned and backed up so that, in the event of an accident, it can be restored into a clone of your original body.

I guess, to be precise, I should say that being resurrected is the easy bit. I don't suppose my original self enjoyed his share of the experience so much; I hear he fell onto the tracks at King's Cross and got dragged halfway to Liverpool Street before the driver noticed. But that was his problem, not mine.

The actual moment of death isn't one of my memories. I'd probably feel differently about it if it were. The last recollection I have from my previous incarnation is going for my regular six-monthly backup and the technicians enclosing my skull in the gleaming bulk of the so-called soul-scanner – the machine that records the state of every single neuron in your brain and packs it all away on a crystal the size of a thumbnail. The next thing I know is that it's a different machine, different technicians, and I have a new body.

And what a body! One moment I'm old and doddery, with a bad knee and a back that complains about the surplus load around my waist. The next, I have the physique of an athlete. My clone was grown from a couple of cells from my old body and rapidly matured in a vat to the equivalent of about age twenty-five. As it grew, its muscles were stimulated by tiny electrical impulses so that, by the time it was decanted, it looked ready to go posing on the beach. Hell, it's fitter than my first body was at that age, since by then I'd already formed a love affair with the high life.

Of course, I'm not the first person to go through this. Anyone who can afford the premiums can be resurrected. But some resurectees get quite sentimental about their previous selves and sometimes even hold services or build monuments to their memories. I don't get it: why bother? Me – who I am – is alive; the thing that died was someone else. That's the end of it.

And now I'm home for the first time since the accident.

For some reason I don't understand, there's been some kind of delay in getting me resurrected – the stupid cow in the crypt couldn't make head nor tail of my case notes, or claimed she couldn't – so the apartment has stood empty for the last six months. On top of which, when my first incarnation had gotten himself sliced and diced by the five forty-five, the previous backup had been something like four months old, so there are changes to the place that I don't recognise. It seems that Mark 1 me decided to paint the sitting room in shades of slate grey, with eggshell blue touches here and there, presumably to add a bit of class. The word, I suppose, is tasteful. Good enough for the old fart I used to be, but not so suitable for my revitalised, man-about-town persona.

I prowl around, looking for other changes, and find, beside the bed, a basket of fruit with a card propped in front of it. I assume whoever was responsible for cleaning the place had accepted delivery and put it there. Carelessly too, for the card is oddly crumpled.

I picked it up and read it, though I can already guess the contents: a message from Great Aunt Matilda, wishing me well and expressing the hope that I will learn from past mistakes.

Sanctimonious old crow! I crush the card in my fist and toss it aside. She might have had the decency to die in the past ten months.

When she'd announced that she wasn't going to take out Resurrection Insurance herself, I'd publicly wept and implored her to reconsider. Well, I'd had to: I can't afford the premiums myself, and paying for them is the only support the old bat gives me, believing I would only squander anything more. Privately, I'd rubbed my hands in anticipation. When she dies, she won't be coming back to resume her tight-fisted clutch on her fortune and, as her only relative, I expect to cop the lot.

Now, with a body ready for action, but without the wherewithal to obtain it, I fret at the sheer wastefulness of the ancient harridan sitting in decaying splendour while refusing to pass on her wealth to those who could make best use of it. If, in the time between my own initial death and the present, she had turned up her toes, I would now be as rich as Croesus and as happy as Larry, whoever they are. As it is, there is a good chance that – since the bureaucrats have already cottoned on to this quirk of resurrection – the most action my young, fit, virile body will be seeing is when I'm conscripted into some government climate scheme, like rebuilding the coastal defences against the next incursion of the sea, or trying to plant oak trees in the Highlands, neither one of which excites me.

I go through to the bedroom, strip off, and admire my new body in the mirror. How crass that such a perfect form should be worn down by mere labour. I search the wardrobes for something decent to wear, frustrated at the lack of choice suitable for someone who wants to dance the night away and return home in the morning with a young lady on each arm. The prospect awakens long forgotten hungers and youthful stirrings and when I look again in the mirror I resolve that this fine, upstanding specimen of manhood will not go to waste.

Sure, I've got two or three lady friends of my own age who I call up from time to time. They're nice enough people to take for a meal and reminisce with about old times. They've even been concerned enough about me to leave notes and messages for my return. But honestly? Now that I'm young again? You think I'm going to fritter away my energy on the likes of them?

If only Matilda would have the consideration to die.

The thought bounces around inside my skull , inexorably evolving from wishful thinking to firm resolution: if the old bat won't die by herself, then I'd better give her a helping hand.

Now, don't get me wrong. I'm not as callous as I might seem. The thought of actually arranging the old biddy's death repels me; she doesn't deserve to be killed, not really. And, of course, there's always the chance of getting caught. The cost of keeping a prisoner indefinitely is too high these days: the penalty for murder is death: permanent death; no resurrection. Which, of course, the insurance companies love, since then they get to keep all premiums. And that really is what everything in the world boils down to: money.

So, Great Aunt, I'm sorry, but my life and needs are vastly more important than yours. It's just a question of making sure I get to enjoy the profits of your demise.

My first plan is simple: a car crash in which both Matilda and I are killed. No one will suspect that of being murder, now will they? Certainly not by me. But when I'm resurrected again, I'll inherit everything.

Except, of course, it won't actually be me. Just as I feel disassociated from my former self, I cannot really empathise with my subsequent incarnation. He'll simply be some other lucky so-and-so, and why the hell should I sacrifice myself for him?

But, but, but ... Half-formed ideas tumble around in my mind. There's me, and there's my next incarnation; what if I could somehow wangle it so that he ended up dead while I lived?

It's the seed of an idea, no more, but I turn it over in my mind until it begins to germinate and blossom. First, I would need to create the illusion that I had died in the same fatal accident that killed Great Aunt Matilda. That could be arranged, I'm sure: I'll need a body of course, then maybe something like a fire fierce enough to obscure any betraying traces of DNA or other distinguishing details. Unless the authorities are suspicious, they won't check too closely, I'm sure. I make a note to investigate the exact procedures they use.

Fuelled by the certainty that my scheme is coming together, I feel the need to celebrate and go over to the cupboard where I keep my drinks, to toast my progress. There's a bottle of fine brandy there, kept for special occasions, or should be unless the lost tail end of my previous incarnation had something to celebrate. In fact, the level in the bottle has dropped considerably. I suppose I should be pleased for the old fart that he had something to make him happy during his last few months, but to be honest, I feel increasingly alienated from my former self and resent him drinking my best brandy.

I pour a hefty measure and recline back in my favourite armchair. The brandy is rich and aromatic, and I savour the first mouthful, appreciating anew the subtle play of flavours. But even my taste buds, it seems, have been regenerated, and I discover in the fiery liquid a bitter after-taste I had not previously noticed. Not everything, it seems, is enhanced by sharper senses and as I sit quietly I discover that even the sounds from the street below, barely audible to older ears, now impinge acutely on my awareness. I am sure it is churlish to bemoan the good fortune of revitalised senses, but once Matilda's millions are under my control I will be able to afford better soundproofing. Or, of course, move somewhere else entirely.

I bring my thoughts back to the plan at hand: disposing of Matilda without getting caught. Where can I get a corpse to substitute for my own body? Well, that would be easy enough. There are so many climate refugees from southern Europe that no-one can keep track of them any longer. I could drive around the slum camps and lure away any number of men of the same build and age as myself. It would be another murder of course, but not of anyone important.

I mustn't be seen after the crash, either; that would give the game away. But the same slum camps that provided a suitable body would provide a suitable refuge. All I'd have to do is hide out and wait for my next incarnation to be decanted.

And then?

Then I would pounce, eliminate him and take over. For a moment - just a moment - I toy with the notion of letting my replacement self live, and of sharing my new life with him. But why?

I will have to be careful though. My new self must never suspect that he is about to be removed. I mustn't update my backups before putting the plan into action, otherwise he will be aware of the scheme as soon as he is resurrected. He must think he is the first restoree, and be totally unaware of what is going to happen to him.

I laugh quietly; it will be a cruel trick to play on myself – I hope I will have a sense of humour about it.

The entrance to the apartment clicks open and I turn my head towards the hallway door in alarm, but cannot see anyone. 'Who's there?' I call, and try to rise from my chair. The brandy must be stronger than I remember, or this body hasn't yet learned how to cope with alcohol, because my arms feel as weak as strands of limp spaghetti, and I collapse back. 'Who's there?' I call again, my heart pounding. 'Speak, damn you!'

A figure steps into view and I know in an instant what has happened and that the brandy has been drugged.

'And do you?' the figure with my face says as it pulls something black and sinister from its pocket. 'Have a sense of humour?'

The fact of the matter is: I don't.

Ashley Jacob

Ashley Jacob is 28 years old and lives in Bath. He grew up in Wrexham, North Wales, where he obtained degrees in Multimedia, Media Studies and Moving Image. Writing has been a lifelong passion; his first piece of literary success was in June 2007 when he won the monthly prize for the *Spinetinglers.com* short horror story contest. He hopes to add the last touches to his sci-fi novel and land it in the hands of professionals for further scrutiny, hoping they either won't get too angry, or at least see the funny side.

Conservation of Angular Momentum

Even for my intensely intoxicated and feckless withered brain, this is a surprise… By all rights I should be dead… Surely I should not just be dead but in smouldering pieces… Speaking of which, what's this coming towards me???

The Circus, directly ahead, perfectly circular, a flattened tripod broken by three evenly spaced lines. Off to the left: the Royal Crescent. Further left from that: Victoria Park. (That's where we started.) Some way off the right: Henrietta Park, the Rugby Ground further south. Just yonder is the Cricket ground. Westerly from this: The Roman Baths, then the Abbey Church. Right at the bottom: The newly appointed Southgate shopping centre. Trace a line from there, back to The Circus, and somewhere in all of that is the Lamb and Lion. (That's where we started started.)

I am spinning. No clue how that's happened. The explosion should have killed me. But I know I'm still alive, and instead of plummeting like some kind of suicidal bird of prey, directly downward, I'm spiralling like a power drill, the city below twirling like a confused compass all around me, north becoming south, becoming northwest, all those iconic landmarks orbiting my reddened flapping face like the planetary cycles of our solar system sped up to the ratio of one earth year for every second, probably more land filling my vision in these infinitesimal instances than for months on end.

No seriously. What is that?

Red… Solid… Metal… Oh… Right… Okay… This'll probably be it then…

Spinning clockwise… Like water down a plughole???

Sam, late forties-my age, ate his share of the pies, holds up a recently appropriated wallet. He draws out two pink vouchers, looks at them curiously, and exits the bathroom.

Bill, the beardy old man farts merrily in the cubicle beside me.

Hands drenched in cold water, I slap my face, take one last look at my dilapidated expression in the mirror and leave the gents. No more staring down plug holes, Lee. Pick up some pride!! Take control!

Pah!!!

Lamb and Lion, every hour some kind of cruelly ironic happy hour. Sam, my good friend and trusted colleague has successfully smashed the moral compass of stealing a stranger's wallet. Apparently, he was a "Plum Twat" who shouldn't have been so keen to leave his stuff by the bar if he cared about it that much. Beverages all round in celebration of this petty crime, more empty glasses than a tired old tosspot like me can possibly count. A Sunday stock up, before the gruelling week ahead that will consist of, well… Nothing… Job??? Hooo, no! I had my chances.

So somehow we get onto the subject of tornadoes. How? Who knows? Can hardly feel my own face.

'… It's just a cloud acting gay…'

I'm inexplicably offended.

'… Something to do with the moon's gravity…'

'No…'

Sam: A good friend. Notorious idiot. In other ways, smarter than me. Luckier, definitely.

'… It spins around in an anti-clockwise direction…'

'No…'

'… Like how water spirals down a plughole. And that's why you only get tornadoes in America. Because they only ever spin anti-clockwise…'

'No NO NO!!!' I slam my fist on the bar. Karl the barman, earliest of twenties, good looking, no nonsense type even in his youth, calls my name. I'm oblivious because I'm shouting.

'Sam… What are you babbling on about?'

'LEE!'

Karl grabs my attention, indefinitely this time, firm lowered eyes like the paternal forewarning to a clip round the ear if I don't get my act together. He'll never be a drunken mess by the age of fifty. This is only a day job to him. I'd better do as he says and lower the tone. This isn't the first time he's told me off… today.

'I saw it on a documentary.'

'No you didn't,' I respond in discreet acknowledgment to my yellow card. 'That's bollocks. They come from storm clouds… The updrafts of low pressure air are so powerful… urpp… they form vortexes… Chances are the vortex will spiral downward, towards the earth… That's a tornado!!!'

I then proceed to waffle on about the Coriolis Effect, the rotational effect on matter, often determined by the earth's hemispheres, and how tornadoes don't just happen in America. There have been tornadoes in Birmingham, for crying out loud.

'Prugh!!!' says farty old Bill. 'There he is. Old Lee-Sharp.'

A term I forgot existed. I continue with misplaced empowerment. 'And the scientific force that maintains the structure of this perpetually spinning object is called… The Conversation… Conversion…. The…'

I lose my wind from my sails.

'No… The…'

'Conversation… Conversion!!! ' cuts in Sam, laughing. 'Are the tornadoes chatting and playing rugby now?'

(Whatever… As long as that force remains, the object in question will spin in a fixed state?!?)

Bill laughs loudly, a worn vocal rasp that bounces around the walls of my skull 'No… I mean…' Oh, shit it! The moment's gone. Good while it lasted. Sam pats me on the back again. I'm sulking. 'We nearly had him there, didn't we. The good old days, yeah???'

Yup. Good they were. Lee-Sharp: My nickname. Full of random but well researched trivia for that lively pub banter. Smart, strapping… Good looking…

… Successful…

… 21 years old. A gorgeous girlfriend. Further down the blurry line of life, I look at her 4 months pregnant. How long ago, I could not tell. How old am I now? 48? 49? Are we still in the Lion?

I go to clink in tribute to those best days. But my glass is empty. Story of my life. Never enough. You always need just one more swig. Forget the love, the respect the ambitions, and that enormous brain you used to have. It was always about the bottle. And now the bottle's all about you. Where is the ex-wife these days? Wish I knew…

My eyes well up. Control over my emotions is in question.

Sam's already going for the refill. Two more lagers. Bill requests a double Jameson's. Sam says 'three of those.'

'Three?'

'Come on! One life.'

As Sam pays with stolen cash, Bill props up by the bar. His worn old eyes look at me. Wisdom beyond his years… An avenue in which to confide? I try...

'If I could find her, Bill…' I mumble, 'I'd give it one good go, one last final - all or nothing chance. But she won't even tell me her address.'

Something of a light sympathetic smile appears behind that beard.

'I used to have so much ahead of me... Then it all went wrong… And I've been stuck in this spiral ever since… It wasn't supposed to be this way…'

For the past thirty or so years, I have been convinced of this fact, a gut instinct more rooted than the one when you wake up and you've soiled yourself.

The old man raises one hand. I listen carefully. One word to start with.

'Enough…'

Sam slides across the deathly booze.

'… Enough… Enough, I cry… A glass, at last… I'm satisfied…'

He bursts out laughing, then drinks his drink. Then he farts again. Sam laughs and drinks his. I put my head down, wipe my eyes and drink mine.

Something happens. Karl refuses to serve us any more.

Bath, springtime: Sunlight reflects off the sand-coloured Roman buildings. The bustling city centre shines like gold, fiery yellow contrasted with rich colours of green. Parks are in clear abundance, virtually impossible to look in a direction and not find a tree of some kind enriching your vision. Bath: Competitively beautiful. Except now those architecturally gratifying forms are discordant blobs of colour mixed with tangled lines. They spill through my retina like acidic liquid. I tumble forth. My stomach turns. I'm feeling suddenly so vulnerably agoraphobic. Sam marches beside me. He's smoking a cigar. Where the hell did he get those?

We stumble our way between buses and people, up towards Queen Square. New avenues are considered. Sam intends to return to the booze without delay. I'm not putting up a fight, fearful my sobriety will return to heartlessly remind me of the relentless travesty that is my life. Flan O'Briens: The owner is standing outside, arms folded, his gaze cutting through mine with a clear enough message. Access denied. The rest: A blur, Sam kicking up a fuss, me engaging in some mild futile intervention, someone pushing me. I stumble straight into a lamppost. Cut to O'Neill's: Really? Already? Sam bangs on the door. Is it shut? Is he barred? How should I know? Next thing I realise, I'm face down on concrete, some bystander pulling me out onto the pavement before my head is crushed under the weight of a speeding taxi. Sam in the distance: Pissing in the centre of Queen Square. Then he's hugging me and jumping on my back. I fall to the floor again. We carry on.

Left at The Circus, unfathomably expensive houses hugging me in mockery from all around. Then, a road that seems to take forever. I unexpectedly buckle left, falling down a flight of concrete steps. Sam is laughing. He's singing the theme tune to Beadle's About. I'm singing along with him, our unruly chanting descending upon the Royal Crescent, where space opens out to impossible dimensions. I throw up on myself. It's boiling hot and we're still wearing our jackets.

A semi ring of gold surrounding a matt of green, a bustle of life, thriving off the sunlight. Distracted, I slam face first into an old red phone box. Then Sam and I storm the gates. Frisbees and footballs dart across my vision like sunspots, more people and voices than is surely appropriate, whole clusters of people, shorts and bikinis galore, families with kids, young couples carefully watching over their younger, loving embraces, arms around each other, lying, sitting, drinking in composed measure, energetic sports types darting in competitive formations. Sam wrestles me to the ground and tickles my ribs, whilst making the noise of a deranged serial molester. I laugh loudly, like a hysterical child, my arms and legs flailing uselessly like I'm an inverted turtle, my chuckles mixed in with jumbled swear words that I scream shamelessly, and as Sam's fingers dig harder into my waist, the tempo of my voice rises to that of one of the nearby college girls who might have been shot by her boyfriend with a water gun. Or maybe one of those little babies, cackling at their own excitement at being able to stand upright for the very first time, at their parents' delight. 'GET OFF ME!!!!' I yell in protest with everything I've got, but still laughing. 'YOU BENT FLABBY PRICK! GET OFF ME YOU FAT FU…'

Sam suddenly relents, moving out of my vision. I'm looking up at the clear blue sky. A blond bombshell wearing only a lacy pink bra floats into my vision. From my own perspective, she is staring only at me.

I pick myself up, my coat covered in grass and sick. 'Woooooo!!!' Sam has seen it too. He turns to me, and leans into my ear.

'Good timing.'

He walks off. Obviously, I'm supposed to follow. First I look up. Bra Lady is moving away, airborne. She is still looking and smiling at me. I turn back to Sam.

Surely not…

We hide before a clearing within Victoria Park. In the distance, a team of people unload a van full of equipment, the crux of their apparatus, a giant basket and an impeccably wide red sheet.

'This must be ours. How about that!'

My head begins to ache: Too much sun and not enough liquid.

'Our what?'

'You remember I bagged Plum Twat's wallet in the Lion? Well I found these.'

This isn't a joke. That's what chills me to the bone. In front of my badly functioning eyes, Sam holds what genuinely appears to be two pink vouchers for a hot air balloon ride.

'You see the names? Percy Ellis for this one, and Vivian Ellis for this. Must have been him and his wife. Ha ha! You remember The Young Ones? Vivian can be a bloke's name as well. We can be brothers!!!'

I gaze carefully at the voucher assigned by default to me. It reads "MRS VIVIAN ELLIS."

'Sam… Not gonna happen mate... They'll probably take one look at us and phone the police… if anything.'

'Take your coat off!'

'What?'

'We put on our sober faces and give it a try. Come on, it'll be fun.'

'It won't work.'

'Listen! You always said you wanted to do something different, and I'm treating you coz your life is crap. Now stop being a drip!'

So, I'm following him across the field, my hot, vomit-basted jacket left out of sight. Sam takes the lead, greets one of the workers as though he'd been nowhere but at home drinking PG tips.

'Hi, I hope we're not too late for the ride. Got stuck in traffic.'

Not a slur in his voice. How does he do that? I stay quiet and let him do the talking.

Our man checks the tickets, gives me a funny look. Sam laughs and polishes up. 'Yeah, automated systems mistake my brother for a girl quite a lot. We should shorten it just to "Ian"…'

The whole process takes about twenty minutes. I try my best to act normal, Sam cheerfully blabs his way into likeability. The balloon men haul a bottle of bubbly and a couple of glasses into the basket. Drinking is allowed. Thank Christ. Better not be sick again though.

A flame spurts up at regular intervals. Hot air gradually fills up the super-strong nylon envelope. Buoyant forces are exerted upon it and we lift off the ground, upward, upward more and further up still, until the air becomes cold and the world shrinks beneath us, inebriated and sober, two states of mind now rendered completely irrelevant, as this is like nothing I've ever experienced. Like it or not, my vision begins to clear, the landscape stretching far ahead and folding into one clearly defined arc. I forget all my troubles. In the great tradition of elaborate metaphors, they seem lifted away. I suddenly obtain a happiness I thought had died in the days of my dignity. But then, I am dignified. I'm no longer stumbling or moaning, or shouting or swearing. I'm just watching silently, as my homeland continues to bob steadily downward.

Shame the same can't be said for Sam. Now afloat and security checked, he's chanting and stumbling like a nob again, his large belly hovering at the edge of the basket. He swears profanities to the unsuspecting public below. I worry that's he's going to start spitting or worse. Instead he pulls out a bottle of Navy Rum. Where in the…

He takes a dose, then hands me the bottle. The pilot is looking at me funny. I smile and shrug. The champagne is gone. Time for the big swig.

The world: Spinning once again.

The now jittery pilot: Bombarded with verbal bollocks, our rendition of Beadle's About taken to a whole louder level. Then I'm in the middle of a conversation rather than the beginning. More unaccounted minutes.

'Sam! What are you waffling on about now?'

'Ha ha… Check this out!'

A rig of propane tanks lining one side of the basket: Sam all out messing with the valves.

'Sam! What are you… Stop it!'

'I'm just doing that thing… You know that makes yer voice go squeaky.'

Sam: A dumb stocky bull. He struggles free of the pilot's grip, yanks at something. Gas and droplets of liquid spurt out. He leans in to inhale the jet.

'That's helium, you dickhead!!!'

Sam, pulls back, his face is a sort of bluish red. He gasps like he's being strangled, then makes a noise that sounds like Elmo from Sesame Street projectile vomiting. He claws at his tongue and rubs his teeth, his scrunched expression a spasm-like fixture.

'Gimme something to drunk!' he coughs. The Navy's empty, so is the bubbly. He fumbles in his jacket for any kind of relief.

'There's nothing left, you idiot!!!'

Sam, so dumb he should have died a thousand times over, yet never a gravestone needed. A miracle of life. All I do is watch. The fumbling.

The search over: The reach for the cigars. The subsequent flick of a cheap lighter…

My ears ring.

Now I'm no longer in the balloon but miles from it. The basket sports a sizeable gap that I can see, even from here. The pilot fondles at emergency procedures. Sam dangles off the edge, clinging on for dear life at 10,000 feet, his flaming trousers falling free of his kicking legs. I'm tumbling downward, not falling straight, but spiralling, caught in a whirlpool doomed to take me to my demise.

But now I think about it, what of it? Certainly fits the pattern. Just a self-made loser hitting the cold unmoving floor of the earth with deservedly bludgeoning force!!!

Then something joins me in my rapid dizzy descent. What be this now? Red… Solid… Metal… Another abandonee of the balloon, another propane tank. From its severed valve, the tiniest flicker of hot purple.

Oh…

Another explosion. Definitely deaf this time. I'm catapulted into a whole new direction, flying sideways, off course, no longer spiralling, going straight, still falling.

A brand new course.

Land… The end…

The Circus: A giant tree. Leafy branches smack me like angry palms. The last thing before instant death… Surely…

An excruciatingly painful snag, my leg snared, impaled on wood perhaps. My trajectory suddenly halted, the force of this emergency stop, the whole bone joint dislocating free of the pelvis… Ouch…

I hang there upside down… How long? Pah!!! Who cares about the time when your life has sucked for the past three decades?

Then, through one of those unimaginably expensive properties surrounding The Circus, a woman stares at me through a window, flabbergasted.

Surprised, I grin... Oh… Long time no see…

Claire King

Claire King was born in Yorkshire and now lives in the French Pyrenees with her husband and two daughters. *Wine at Breakfast* is one of a collection of short stories, set in Ukraine, which she is tweaking and polishing. Claire has also recently finished her first novel, currently in the third round of judging for the *Brit Writers' Awards 2010*, and is preparing it for submission this summer. A graduate of Newnham College, Cambridge, Claire works independently, helping organisations collaborate. She is active in the online writing community, including *Fictionaut* and *Metazen*. This is her first published work.

Wine at Breakfast

That morning there had been a scandal in the kitchen. Lena's parents' angry whispers behind closed doors. Her mother's stifled weeping.

'She's fourteen! Fourteen! It's the worst time, Oleg.' Glasses and bottles slammed.

'What do you want me to do, Valya, break her legs?'

Lena's father had emerged, sweating, and handed her a wine glass, full to the brim. 'Drink.'

The wine was starting to wear off now, thank God. It made her knees sleepy, no good for marching. Lena forced her arms to swing stiffly by her sides, fighting the urge to scratch her head. The spring air wasn't right: not fresh and clean but dry and dusty. She hadn't been able to get her hair clean all week no matter how much soap she'd used. As she marched past the football stadium and onto the Boulevard her heart pounded against the tails of her Young Pioneer neckerchief. The sight ahead was overwhelming. As usual, the whole of Kiev had turned out for May Day, thronging both sides of the vast Boulevard. Thick fanfares of tall coloured flags punctuated the roadside, fluttering in the wind. It was a strong one today, billowing through the corridor of municipal buildings and scattering chestnut blossom confetti over the parade.

Most spectators saw nothing out of the ordinary. The city was adept at concealing its fear. Only if you knew, you could finger the differences - a few men a little drunker than usual, a few eyes glancing up uneasily at the dark clouds moving in from the North. Oleg and Valya watched the rainclouds rolling in, felt the wind creep over their skin. But they stood steadfast in the swelling tide of bodies, forcing sharp smiles, waiting to see Lena march. Oleg held tight to Valya's hand. To her other side her parents' smiles were genuine and full; May Day in Kiev was a great spectacle, and they were just pleased to be out of danger. Although it was Igor and Anya who had brought news of the fire to them last week, Oleg had insisted they should not know the truth.

Their call had come on Saturday morning. The air, almost summery, was blowing through the open windows, carrying a gift – the scent of newly blooming lilac – into the apartment. Oleg was playing Beethoven. Valya had answered the phone.

'Hello, Papa,' she said.

'I need to talk to Oleg,' said her father. 'There were noises in the night, and there's a fire at the plant. Your mother is scared.'

'Oleg! Come please!' Valya called.

The piano stopped abruptly, Oleg's footsteps on the parquet. Valya relaying the news and Oleg's scowl.

'Wait. I'll check.' Oleg went to the cupboard where he kept his work supplies. He came back with a Geiger counter clutched against his chest and snatched the phone from Valya.

'Ok, Igor,' he said, 'pack a couple of bags. I'll come for you.' There were muffled protests on the other end of the line.

'Igor, listen,' Oleg smiled up at Valya, 'I am coming now. I won't be long.'

Then he was on her. Up close and urgent. 'Valya,' Oleg's face was almost touching hers, his hand grasping her shoulder, 'Where's Lena?'

Valya shifted uneasily. 'She's gone for a walk with her friends in town.'

Oleg shivered. 'You stay here and clean the floors. When Lena comes back, she can help you. And close the damned windows.'

'The windows?' Valya frowned. 'You know they haven't turned the heating off yet. We'll roast.'

'Valya,' Oleg raised the Geiger counter in front of her face, raised his voice too, 'look at it. It's filthy!'

The needle almost leapt off the scale. Valya gasped, one hand shot to her mouth and the other flew out to steady herself against the wall. 'Oleg!' she cried. 'Lena!'

Oleg gestured fiercely with his eyes towards the living room wall, a thin partition from their neighbours. He shook his head and raised his voice. 'OK I'm off now, Sweetheart. See you later!'

'Bye, Honey.' Valya replied.

It was an eerie road north, although nothing was notably different. Traffic came and went. Oleg passed several families driving out to their dachas, cars loaded high with boxes and crates. As he approached Chernobyl village, still some distance from the plant, the militia waved him down. His temples pulsed as he came to a halt.

'Documents?' The sallow-faced recruit held out a gloved hand. Oleg handed over his papers without a word. The policeman glared at them. 'Where are you going?' he asked.

Oleg rolled his eyes. 'Collecting my in-laws for the weekend,' he said.

A pause, then the documents were thrust back through the car window.

'You'd be better off fishing.' The policeman waved his baton at Oleg with a sneer and walked away.

The air in Chernobyl smelled of orange blossom. More militia lazed around in the sunshine by the fountain, smoking cigarettes, telling dirty jokes. Children chased barefoot through the village street, back and forth to the stream, trailing muddy footprints in their wake. The sun was high and scorched his face, but Oleg was cold to the bone.

'We don't want to be any trouble,' said Anya, loading various bags into the car, 'but you can see the fire.' She pointed out across the marshlands to the reactor. A few flames flickered through a damaged wall, one chimney glowing like an ember.

'You're no trouble,' said Oleg, hurrying her along.

'In the bread shop,' said Anya, 'nobody mentioned it.' She turned to Igor. 'I wondered if we should stay in the house and wait to see what the militia say.'

'How can we stay in the house,' said Igor, 'when the toilet is outside?'

'I think it is better if you come to Kiev,' said Oleg. 'Let's go.'

Anya locked the door to her little whitewashed cottage and climbed into the car.

That night, when Igor and Anya had retired to Lena's room and Lena slept on the sofa, Oleg and Valya camped at the kitchen table. Oleg poured red wine into vodka glasses.

'What do we do?' whispered Valya.

'What can we do?' said Oleg.

'There must be some way...'

'OK. Let me think.' Oleg rubbed at his forehead. 'Right, we have to eat pickles.'

'Pickles?'

'And dried sausage. No fresh vegetables, milk, anything that could be... you know.'

'Pickles and sausage, right.' Valya's eyes were wide and blurred with tears, 'and then, what will we breathe?'

Oleg dropped his head into his hands. For a while they said nothing. 'Valya,' he said eventually. 'You know we have to carry on as normal.'

'I can't let Lena go out there, Oleg. I can't do it.'

'If we haven't been told, it's because they don't want us to know. What do you think they would do if we let slip? They know I have the equipment, Valya, they'll be watching.'

'We could keep Lena off school, say she's sick?'

'It's too risky. But at least we should stay away from the river and out of the rain. And when we come home we will wash. Our clothes, our hair, our skin...' Oleg reached over and stroked Valya's wrist with his index finger. He refilled their glasses. 'The wine will make the radiation pass through faster,' he whispered.

That night, Valya cried out for Lena so loud in her sleep that Oleg had to press his hand to her mouth and shake her awake.

All week, Kiev simmered on rumours, fuelled by a rash of unexplained events. The buses had all disappeared from the streets, the firemen too. There had been a run on suitcases in the central department store and an unusual spate of last minute holidays to the Black Sea. The sun shone, the birds sang but something was definitely awry. People wanted answers. The night before May Day there was a television broadcast. Lena's family watched it together, cramped up in the small stuffy living room with Igor and Anya. There had been a fire at the reactor, it said, but it was nothing to be concerned about. No danger. The May Day Parades were expected to be better than ever this year. Anya got up and left the room.

The itch on Lena's scalp was driving her crazy and now the wine had worn off she was starting to feel sick. As she reached October Revolution Square she rolled her eyes roadside, anxiously searching out her mother's face in the place they had agreed. This morning, after the fight in the kitchen, her mother had been a wreck. Her hands were shaking so much she spilled her wine. Wine, at breakfast? Lena feared the worst, whatever that might be. But no, there was her mother's face at last, beautiful and composed in the shifting crowd, meeting Lena's eye and smiling warmly. Lena took a deep breath, filling her lungs, and smiled back, calmed. Everything was OK after all.

When Lena turned her eyes front again, Valya's smile stayed in place a fraction too long. It started to rain.

Nastasya Parker

Nastasya Parker grew up in New Hampshire, USA, and now lives in Gloucestershire with her husband and young son. Although she has a degree in Writing and Literature, this is her first published work. She works in a nursing home and as a waitress, gathering story ideas and hoping for a moment to replant them.

The Meek Inherit

My family made the best mud cakes in Cité Soleil. Papa's dirt, Maman's measuring, my mixing - little wonder the neighbour children would snatch drying cakes from our tin roof. One day they brought the whole tin sheet clanging down. My brother Jackson and I helped Maman balance it back onto our walls. But a batch of mud-cakes had splattered to the ground, leaving her with no Tè to sell to the famished mothers and babies at market that week. No earth.

I surveyed the fragments, still squidgy at the edges. I put my hands on my hips. Through my checked green school dress, the bones fit into my grasp. 'Imbeciles,' I spat. When I steal Tè, I stand on crates. I don't have someone launch me onto a flimsy shack top.

'They're children, Mariette,' Maman sighed. She adjusted the cloth that bound my baby brother to her back, then continued rationing rice for us. We would have smaller portions until she could return to market with cakes to sell. There was the ruined Tè, of course, but while we prefer eating salted mud to starving, we know our limits. Children must not live by earth alone.

'I'm their age, and I'm smarter than that.'

'You are lucky,' she corrected me, as always. 'An American sponsors you to go to school. You were better fed when you were young, and the Marines were here. You owe this to Providence, so mind it does not take any back.'

But I didn't see it that way. Did God, or spirits, take away the food aid? No, gangs scared off the Haitian police and the U.S. Marines. With no one to give out mosquito nets, did God drop them from the sky? Ha. I found an old tarp, pinpricked it hundreds of times, and rigged it over the little ones' nest of blankets. And when rice and beans became too expensive, I suggested buying a cheap mud cake for each of our small crying children.

Papa objected to my idea of filling the babies' swollen bellies with mud, and threatened to beat us, just that once. But Maman had cried, 'We had no choice!'

'You think I can't get money for food?'

'No one can.'

He left our shack then, and when he returned weeks later, he was stooped, guiding a wheelbarrow with each hand. Papa had walked to the Hinche Plateau for pale, clean earth. 'Do what you must,' he said.

So we began our business. Maman used my makeshift mosquito net to sift the yellow dirt free of bugs. She poured in the cleanest-looking water she could find, added oil on top, and sprinkled in salt. I scoured the trash-packed streets for plastic to fit over my feet; old rice sacks, or split oil jugs. Then I stomped the ingredients into mud. The first minutes were best, before it became heavy and hot like everything else. Once the mud was mixed, Maman and I slapped it down in balls and patted it into Tè. She laid her pies on our roof to dry, counting to see I hadn't stolen one.

Not that I steal her mud cakes, of course! I take from rival saleswomen, though some use filthy brown Port-au-Prince earth. Few have a man like my Papa in the family, traveling to the Plateau. He brings mud weekly or monthly, depending on whether he has found jobs in the city, and whether he has worked up enough strength to set eyes on us.

'You're no better than us,' some children would taunt me. 'Your Papa's gone.'

'My Papa comes back.' I walked past with my tightly braided head held high.

'Mine's always here,' said one girl, her hair glowing red from lack of food.

'Too bad for you,' I said. 'He's a drunk, I hear him shout at your Maman.' She was one of the rival saleswomen.

'Mine protects our Cité.' This boy pointed his scabby fingers like a gun.

Protects! Ha. A gang member, then. Who made us pay fees and gave food only sometimes in return. But I knew better than to say anything, so I carried on walking. And later, doubled back to steal some of their mothers' drying mud cakes.

Because I am an expert in the uses of mud, trash, and all things Cité Soleil, I eat only half when I get a mud cake. The other half I use wet. I chop the Tè and creep away with half on each hand to the sewage pond. From crate to tyre I leap, letting them drift me to the centre. Then I sit my bottom on the rim of a tyre, perch my feet opposite, and lay one half of my mud pie to dry next to me. The other half I lather over my arms and neck and feet to soothe my sun-cracked skin. I'm plagued by mosquitoes and always sporting a burn here, a rash there; thanks to bathing in the toilet water of chickens, goats and people alike. Where else is there to do it? My shantytown may lie by the sea, but it's built on a huge, shifting rubbish heap. I can't say whether my view of the Caribbean sparkles from natural beauty or from drifting tin cans catching the sun.

I know other tricks, too. Getting sweets from Marines. Mustn't get lost in the crowd of black faces and reaching hands, voices singing, 'Hey yooooouuu! Give me! Bonbon! Ballon!' I would put my hand on a soldier's sweaty wrist and stare into his face. Eventually any soldier would give me candy. I ate quickly, but didn't lick the streaks of melted sugar from the wrapper. I would smooth the plastic into my palm, and cover my face so I could breath sweetness over the stench of my Cité.

The Marines left before I started school. One of my teachers gave sweets, though, to those who were especially smart. Now, maybe the goodness of the spirits and the mercy of God had found me a sponsor to send money for my uniform, this crisp dress the colour of grass, palms and everything else the Cité kills. Their generosity got me through the door of the cinder block school. But I'm the one who memorised times tables, and earned a shining red candy. When I pressed its wrapper, my fingernail sank into the red oval from the heat. I slipped it into my dress pocket as we stood in lines to leave the school, our voices lilting through the national anthem.

Suddenly our queue swayed, then fell to its knees. Like when I stood on a crate to steal Tè and some boys pulled the crate from under my feet. Only now, there was no ground to land on, though my shoes, tight around the toes, were still on the floor! I heard a noise louder than gunfire, thunder so close my heart tripped. Smoke rose around us; I thought UN tanks would crash through our walls. We ran.

Outside, the thunder had broken into bangs more similar to gunfire. The smoke tasted familiar. Dirt, dust; not smoke. The screaming was louder and quieter at the same time. As if more people were shouting, but from further away, or from under blankets. A teacher shouted, 'Tranbleman'd tè!' The earth had shaken.

Had it rebelled, tired of being eaten? I was standing on it now, on a packed mud street swept mostly clean. Still I felt I was falling. Children in green rushed past, and the dust parted to reveal the other side of the street. The school for sponsored children with red uniforms had collapsed. No more two cement storeys with slatted blocks for windows - just heavy rubbish. Every child in the opposite building would have been at study; they were not released until fifteen minutes after we were.

The dust stirred again, closing like a curtain. Would the same happen to our school? I screamed. 'Jackson!'

My voice was lost. So I grabbed wrists, even plaits, of my fellow pupils running by, much more firmly than I would dare catch hold of a Marine. 'Where is Jackson Aimedieu?'

Most gave panicked looks and broke away. Some had grazed knees or cuts elsewhere - one elbow I grasped was sticky with blood.

How long did I stand there, my heart pounding like thunder, dust stinging my eyes, screams tearing my throat? Until one boy cried, 'He's gone home!'

The breath I took felt like my first in hours. I let the boy go, and paused to fill my lungs before running home myself.

Then out of the dust a storm of men careered. Their eyes were wild, chins stubbled, clothes tattered. One ran straight into me. I was sent flying to the other side of the street, like a rag-stuffed sack boys kick for soccer.

I was on the dead side. Dust thickened, then thinned as if I were inside a pumping, choking fist. I put my hands out to pull myself up, and touched rough cement. Pieces of the other school. Some small child was sobbing for his Maman. This heap was a monster with hundreds alive in its belly, scratching, shrieking.

I stood without daring to breathe, lest it hear and devour me too. One ankle no longer worked. I put my hands out to my sides as if I were carrying mud cakes, as if I were stepping across the sewage lake, and moved on tiptoe. I tripped over another fallen brick, and my knee landed on a lesson book. Someone else had been learning times tables.

Up I got again. Will the spirits of dead and dying trap me with the others? No, Mariette, be strong, I told myself; you still have your body, you are free. I lurched forward, halted again. I could see red-checked cloth. One of them had escaped - no, been thrown by the bucking floors, and on top of her more blocks had fallen. I could see her skirt but no legs, and then, as I approached - how could I not approach? - I saw her dark face. Sweat gleaming through dust, but no tears.

'Ede'm,' she croaked, 'help me.'

My hand went to my chest to make the sign of the cross as we were taught at school. What was I doing? How would that help her, even if it made me feel safe? My hand froze against my breast pocket. I remembered the candy inside, already an absurd relic.

I grabbed two men running past, and they strained to lift the chunk of wall on the girl's legs. Muscles bulged in their stick-like arms but they could not move the cement. They ran around the school looking for ways to free the others.

Mothers arrived, dust clinging to their bright skirts and t-shirts, some carrying babies, all wailing. 'Oh God! Who will save our children?'

I remembered Maman, as if she were as foreign as the candy in my pocket. Would she drag the little ones and hurry to find me? I must get to her, I thought, before she sees this. I dropped to my knees by the red-uniformed girl. The sweet clung to its wrapper after I untwisted the crackling ends, but I peeled it off and eased it into her mouth. 'Eat slowly,' I whispered. 'Pretend there is nothing in the world but fruit, sweet and cool.'

She closed her eyes, and seemed to nod. I ran, pushing my thumb against the wrapper in my palm, telling myself there was nothing but smooth plastic; no pain wrenching my ankle, no salty tears mingling with dust in my mouth and eyes.

Running through Cité Soleil, I found the streets more crowded than ever. People were shouting, arms wide. The dust had turned to black smoke. We have no cement houses, but we cook our food on fires outside our shacks. And these fires had spread. Some women clustered around a young mother screaming as badly as the trapped children. I slowed to look, and saw no skin on her arm, just smoking flesh, like a zombie's limb in our old stories. I sped up again. Many shacks were leaning or roofless. The earth had shaken here too.

Our shack still stood, though angled towards the supporting sticks on one side. Papa had pushed them firmly into the rubbish heap, and packed their bases with mud. I saw it from a short distance, the yellow washing tub leaning by the doorway. Jackson stood outside too, holding the baby.

I threw my arms around both of them. 'The school, the red school - did you hear? Where is Maman?'

'Inside.' His voice was so low. 'Delvine and Gessner, they're gone.'

'Our little ones? Where? How?'

'Mariette?'

'Maman?' She looked old, her eyes deep and black and seeing something else. What did I look like now?

'They were on a tyre, on the lake. And the lake swallowed them.' She caressed our heads with the same expression as when she counted her mud cakes.

I had shown them how to reach the tyre. 'Sorry,' I whispered. What a foolish thing to say! Like giving a legless girl a sweet. All these horrible things - they were real. How had I walked on a twisted ankle through this disaster, encouraged only by a sticky scrap of plastic?

Maman smoothed my dress. 'So dirty,' she whispered and shook her head. 'Only you, Mariette.'

I buried my head in her chest, remembering the greater reasons I had dragged myself home.

I threw the candy wrapper, unlicked, into the sewage lake, half in rage, half wanting to give the little ones all I had. Soon I wished I'd found another way to mark their passing, because the smell of Cité Soleil became worse: sickly sweet yet salty with blood. The smell of dead bodies. Some people joked, at least the flies had somewhere else to go.

They returned the bodies to the earth their murderer, together in great human knots. In Titanyen outside the city, cursed land where no one goes. How could anyone, dead or alive, find peace this way?

Mamam sat trying to coax milk for the baby from her parched body 'There's no other choice.' The earthquake had shattered buildings but built up her old excuses to the sky. 'The corpses carry disease on their stink.' Of course, the bodies of our precious ones were somewhere under the lake. Although there was Papa, too ... who knew where he might be.

The sky groaned with planes all day, and at night came silence I hadn't known existed in my Cité. We listened for the gang leaders who had escaped the destroyed prison, and almost wished the UN base in its innocent guise of light blue had not been destroyed also. Jackson and I buried our uniforms under a trash heap, hiding our good fortune so gangsters wouldn't think we had something to give.

On Sunday songs banished the silence. People walked through the streets, arms linked, singing prayer, praise, mourning. Life coursed through our Cité, and my love for it blazed.

Maman watched their flip-flops as they passed, her head bent. 'God punished us, our ancestors in the earth didn't protect us. Who will save us now?'

'We'll save us.' I poured our last oil into a bowl of dust Jackson and I had collected. We'd hoped it would be cleaner than dirt from the ground. The cakes would not help our thirst but might ease the ache in our bellies.

'Mariette. When will you realise how little our lives are worth? If this hasn't proved it -'

'Here, even mud is worth something.'

Food returned before Papa did. Jackson and I waited hours to collect biscuits and bottles of water. That was all for three days, until Papa showed up. He wore a jacket and produced food from its pockets.

He passed Maman a bag of rice. 'Tonight we feast; tomorrow we leave the Cité. We'll get a farm, Vivienne. A few animals, fruit trees ...'

She stared from his beaming face to the rice. 'Where did you get this?'

I stopped slurping the juice he'd brought. We'd heard stories of looters chopped to pieces. Not Papa!

'I bought it. I have money, see? Even if I were a thief, how could I steal a farm?' He embraced her. 'You're tired. These days have been horrible.'

Maman shook free. 'Titanyen.'

His smile vanished, like a crocodile's or a politician's. 'What?'

'You've been digging,' she whispered. 'They say it pays hundreds of gourdes each day, to throw away people as if they never lived.'

'Listen, we have someplace to go now. There's nothing in Port-au-Prince.'

I put my hands on my hips. 'Gessner and Delvine are beneath here, don't you know? And school will open again!'

Maman's voice quivered. 'When you shoveled bodies into the pits, did you check to see if they were ours?'

He backed away. 'I didn't have to; I'd had word.'

'We had nothing!'

'That's why I took the job while I could. It's a new beginning! The spirits helped us at last.'

'By killing thousands, even our little ones? We don't need their help.' She slammed the bag of rice, still sealed, into a corner.

'Woman! Come on. I did this so we can be together.'

'You did this for money.' She turned her back on him. 'No new beginning can come from death money.'

Papa stroked my cheek. His hand felt the same but I thought I smelled death on it. I didn't shrink away, in case it was the last touch he ever gave. He left.

Maman put the food into her storage corner. 'We'll make this last.' She surveyed us, her eyes flickering, her forehead creasing. 'Have I chosen death for us?'

'At least you chose something. You never looked more alive.' I cradled the crying baby. 'Don't worry. Even when there's no food, I always find something to eat.' The earth has taken its fill; it should be our turn now.

Jonathan Pinnock

Jonathan Pinnock has been writing on and off for most of his life but only started taking it seriously in 2007. Since then he has won several prizes for his short stories and poetry as well as being published in a wide range of places including *Litro*, *Every Day Fiction* and *Necrotic Tissue*. He is also responsible for the increasingly peculiar web serial *Mrs Darcy vs. The Aliens*, but hopes that he will be forgiven for that transgression. In real life, he writes computer software and is married with two slightly grown-up children.

rZr and Napoleon

rZr takes the photograph out of his pocket and looks at it one last time. He shakes his head and puts it away again. He adjusts his balaclava and repositions his mask. He puts on a new pair of latex gloves and switches on the airbrush. Once he would have used standard industrial spray cans, but that was back in the day when he was daubing trains. rZr steps back and surveys the wall that is his canvas.

'Edgy,' he says to himself. 'I'll give you fucking edgy.'

The room smells of polish and leather and one wall is taken up with a vast map of the world, covered in pins. There are half a dozen people sitting around the table apart from rZr. He and Miranda are the only ones not wearing suits: Miranda because she is the only woman present and rZr because he is rZr. They are heavily outnumbered but they are calling the shots.

'It really would be much easier to do this if Mr ... rZr ... would remove his balaclava,' the prick from marketing is saying. Miranda glances at rZr. He shakes his head.

'rZr will remain anonymous for the duration of this commission,' she says. 'rZr's anonymity is concomitant with his role as a guerrilla artist and it would not be appropriate for him to break his normal mode of working, even for such an important client as yourselves.'

'It's just that it's ... a bit ... odd having to deal with – '

'You deal with me, as rZr's representative,' says Miranda, noticing rZr's scribbled note saying "CLOSE THE FUCKER DOWN NOW. 'rZr is only here to observe and ensure that he is happy with the way that the negotiations are handled.' She pauses, making sure that she has the agreement of everyone in the room. No-one objects. 'So, if we could continue to point 14.3, creative control. This is particularly important for rZr as there are those who would construe that his integrity as an artist might be compromised by the very act of talking to people such as yourselves – '

'Well, he isn't exactly talking to us, is he – '

'– and it is therefore essential to the success of the project that rZr is allowed to have complete creative – '

'Absolutely,' says the smoothie next to the prick from marketing. He was introduced as being responsible for corporate art procurement, although this is his first contribution to the meeting. 'We have long had a policy here of investing in cutting edge art and we specifically set out to hire rZr as part of this ongoing process. In fact, the mural for the chairman's office is one of the more significant acquisitions that we are likely to make this quarter.'

The prick from marketing raises his eyebrows at this, but the chairman shakes his head. rZr looks hard at him. He knows a surprising amount about the chairman, and very little of it tallies with the charming, physically unassuming man sitting opposite him. When he walked into the room, he was five foot nothing. Small man, big ambition, thinks rZr. Like Napoleon. Now there's an idea.

'I'm with Peter on this,' says the chairman, gesturing at the procurement guy, 'we do this properly. If it's got to be edgy, then edgy it is.'

'But, surely, given the amount we're spending on this – ' says the prick from marketing.

ANY MORE OF THIS AND I'M OFF, writes rZr. FUCK THIS SHIT.

'If I can interject,' says Miranda, 'Maybe if I show you some current selling prices for rZr's work, it might make this discussion irrelevant?' She passes across a piece of paper and all five of them on the opposite side of the table study it with interest.

'We're in the wrong business,' says the prick from marketing. No-one laughs.

'So, if we can move on? The next point concerns the schedule for the transfer of funds into the numbered bank account – '

Usually, he has only the vaguest of ideas about what he's going to paint when he begins work on a wall. But this time, he's thought long and hard about it and he knows exactly what he's going to do. He starts in the middle and paints a large caricature of Napoleon with a bare arse and the chairman's face. Yeah. Nice. Then he starts to work outwards from there. After a while, rZr tightens the strap on his mask as the room begins to fill with solvent fumes.

Miranda and rZr are leaving the building by the underground car park, as specified in the contract. She pauses as they emerge from the liftwell.

'Well, I think we're due a celebration, aren't we?' she says.

'Not yet,' says rZr.

'Jesus Christ, r, we've just screwed over one of the biggest, bastardest corporations in the world. Aren't you happy?'

'No. Not yet.'

She looks at him. 'I don't get you, r. Maybe it's because I can never see your face behind that stupid balaclava, but – '

'Let's just say I'm playing a long game here, and it's not over yet.'

She scrutinises his face again. 'I don't even understand why you're doing this. I don't get it. OK, I guess I understand why you've gone corporate. It happens to everyone eventually. But you still seem – '

'Conflicted? Yeah. Maybe I am. Listen, I'd love to stand here talking to you, but I need to have a bath. Being in that place makes me feel dirty, y'know?'

'Sure … sure. Maybe we'll go for a drink … some other time?'

'Yeah, sure. Maybe. Whatever.'

rZr watches Miranda leave and then heads off in the opposite direction into the backstreets. When he's sure that no-one's looking, he takes off his balaclava and takes a deep breath. Not long now. He emerges into the sunlight and heads off towards the tube. The photograph is burning a hole in his pocket.

rZr is almost finished now. He's pleased with some of the details he's managed to insert in there, especially some of the hidden references to the corporation's covert activities in various mineral-rich African basket cases. rZr has done his research and he knows exactly what he is dealing with here.

The prick from marketing is studying the finished work, glass of wine in hand.

'It's very green, is it not?' he says.

'rZr is working a lot in green at the moment,' says Miranda, improvising. rZr, standing aloof from the rest of the crowd, gives the slightest of nods.

'Well, I don't know a lot about art,' says the prick from marketing. 'Think most of it's a load of bollocks. But I suppose I can see something in it. Not terribly edgy, though, is it, apart from the strange froggy geezer mooning in the middle of it all?'

'rZr says that there are hidden layers in there.'

'Oh, I see. Subtlety. You surprise me. I thought you arty types just liked painting dog turds and stuff like that. Still, Sir Michael seems to like it, so that's all that matters.' He gestures to a waiter. 'Top up, please!'

'Do you ever take the balaclava off?' says Peter from corporate art, sidling over.

'No, he doesn't,' says Miranda. 'Well, I've never seen him without it.'

'Really? How extraordinary. I thought you two were – '

Miranda smiles. 'Er … no … I mean – '

Peter raises an eyebrow and walks away.

'Sorry about that,' says Miranda.

rZr leans close to her and whispers, 'I've had enough of this shit. Let's go.'

She gives him an odd look, and then says, 'OK'. She puts down her drink and follows him out of the room. The rest of the party are watching as Sir Michael discusses various aspects of his new mural with several hangers-on. rZr wonders how soon it will be before the chairman gets the hidden message.

They pause briefly in the corridor outside the chairman's office. It's almost as if she's waiting for him to do something. And Christ knows, he'd like to do it with her, right in that room opposite, right on the fucking boardroom table. But this has never been about pleasure. He shakes his head. He takes the crumpled photograph out of his pocket and hands it to Miranda. She looks at it and stares back at him.

'I've got to go,' says rZr.

The work on the new clinic is going well – and not a moment too soon, as the facilities in the villages nearby can no longer cope with this onslaught of chronic illness. You could be forgiven for wondering which god is taking his vengeance on them, and what they have done to offend him. But even these people, whom circumstance has denied anything other than the most basic of education, know exactly what has caused it.

rZr is almost happy for the first time in years. Provided that the trucks can get through with a few more loads before the rains start, phase one of the project should be completed on schedule. They'll have to wait a few months before they can start on the orphanage, but in Africa you have to work with nature, not against it. And then he has to organise the recruitment of the staff, so he'll need to double-check how many of them the interest on that Swiss account is going to pay for.

His second mobile rings and as ever it amuses him that in Africa you can be eight hours' journey down a dirt track and still pick up a perfect signal. He enjoys ironies like that. The call will have been routed through untraceable forwarding accounts in at least eight other countries to get to him. He recognises the number. He's been waiting for this call.

'Miranda, hi,' he says.

'Er, hi.' She sounds nervous. It's the first time they've spoken for several months.

'So what can I do for you?'

'Christ, you sound a long way away.'

'Maybe, but I bet the weather's nicer here.'

'Listen, r, you know that photograph you gave me?'

'Yeah?'

'The kid in it ... the poor thing ... was it ... arsenic?'

'Yeah.'

'Shit.' There's a long silence. rZr waits.

'There's something I need to tell you,' says Miranda. The tone in her voice has shifted slightly, and rZr's heart skips a beat.

'Yeah?'

'Something odd's happened. Remember Sir Michael whatsit? The chairman?'

rZr can barely breathe. 'Yeah?'

'He's ... he's ... dead.'

He can't help smiling, although his heart is now thumping away like a steam hammer. 'Really? Well, I can't say I – '

'Shut up, r. He's been poisoned. I mean, can you imagine it? And with arsenic, too.'

rZr says nothing.

'r, this isn't something you've done, is it? I mean, I don't know how, but – '

He pauses.

'r?'

He takes a deep breath. 'Did you ever hear the story about how Napoleon died?'

'Sorry?'

'They say he was killed by toxins leaking from his wallpaper. Arsenic compounds.' He looks over towards the new clinic. 'That shit can fuck you up in all sorts of ways, you know. Ask anyone living near the run-off from a mine.'

'You're scaring me, r.'

'But you don't get arsenic in wallpaper any more, do you? Or in paint. Usually. But if you want an extra-specially vivid green, what you really need is Emerald Green.' He pauses. 'Also known as copper acetoarsenate.'

'Oh my God, but that mural – '

He doesn't say anything.

'r?'

'Look, it's probably best we don't talk for much longer. Been good working with you, but I've got things to do.'

'r – '

'As of this moment, I'm not called rZr any more, Miranda. I'm just another nameless guy in Africa. Forget everything you ever knew about me.' With that, he switches the phone off, removes the SIM card and crushes it under his foot. Closure.

And then, walking towards him, emaciated and unsteady on her feet, is the woman in the photograph. Limping next to her is the child that she was carrying in it. His feet are misshapen and turn in on themselves. The woman holds out an unsteady hand to the artist formerly known as rZr.

'Thank you,' she says, bowing.

He shakes his head. He doesn't want her gratitude. He doesn't want anyone's gratitude. It's personal, this, and it always has been. He gives a half smile and turns away from her, in time to see a group of men struggling to unload an operating table from the lorry. 'Hey!' he shouts, 'You take care with that thing.'

Marli Roode

Marli Roode is grateful that she wanted to be a writer, a field in which 26 is still considered to be young(ish). She lives in London, eking out an existence by making verbs out of unsuspecting nouns. Marli recently completed the Creative Writing MA at Manchester University. She won the *Is There A Novelist In The House?* competition at the Manchester Literature Festival as well as the *Mulcahy Conway Prize* for her novel, *Call It Dog*, which is currently under consideration at an agency. She was born in South Africa and really likes dogs.

Spring Tide

The swallows have made their nest in the extractor fan. We woke them with our suitcases and the sound of spoons in coffee cups. Now we sit in the dark because we don't know which switch will turn on the lights and which will blade matted feathers and pulp onto the white living-room walls. We talk quietly about the drive from Cape Town and listen to the birds complain. I wonder what swallows dream about.

Walt and Marie have been here for three days, cleaning dead bees out of sinks and filling labelled bottles with herbs brought down from Pretoria. The couches and coffee table are still under heavy drapes. There is too much salt in the air, Marie will tell me later over a cigarette, and too much light: between visits, ornaments and jars of basil blanch and fade. This is why, she says, they have a system now, why we couldn't come earlier. In those three days, they scoop spiders out of sinks, leave half-smoked cigarettes, ash still in perfect cylinders, all over the house, drive to Jeffrey's Bay to fetch water in five-litre barrels because the borehole water makes bad tea. I try to imagine the colour evaporating out of wood and linen but can only picture cartoon jars turning white, shivering with fear as though an animated hammer had just walked into the room.

Marie is still asleep when we arrive, but Walt has been up since half three waiting for us. I hear half past four, caught out by the same peculiarity in Afrikaans that used to have me rolling my eyes at English classmates. Now, my memory of my first language is good only for the words for elf, spell and magic; I don't know how you would say grown-up words like chemotherapy, mortgage or abortion. My traitor's tongue stumbles over my own name.

Walt had waved from the balcony when we'd pulled up, his dressing-gown fizzing against the grey sky. It looked as though all the gas was nearly out of him. Kicking the blood back into my legs, I wondered if his moustache would still be blonde, up close. Or if it, like his eyebrows, was gone now.

We drink coffee at Marie's mother's yellow-wood table, which is covered in a plastic film to save the wood from jam and vinegar. The curtains are tied back so that we can see the fog drift back out to sea, like a jellyfish on the tide. In front of us, the hill the house is built on falls away into dark green plants, with small leaves and even smaller purple flowers. A potholed tennis court is dark brown with dew. Then the dune, which moves every year, Walt says. This early in the day, it is unmarked and white as butterfat. At the gate to the beach, a light flashes on a yellow pick-up. It'd passed us on the dirt road into the bay, shooting stones up at our windows like children spitting watermelon pips. We'd watched it rocket through the red dust.

'There was a storm the day before yesterday,' Walt says. 'Gale-force winds crying round corners everywhere.' He stands up to measure more coffee in heaped spoons. 'Burt says it'd been absolutely perfect since the beginning of December, all the way until we got here. But he always says that.'

'Burt is the neighbour on that side,' my father explains to me. 'We gave him a copy of The Hitchhiker's Guide for Christmas one year, and he said "No thanks. I don't want that book; I already have one."' We laugh, but Walt starts to cough.

'Don't you want to go back to bed?' my father asks him. 'We can sort out our rooms. I know where the towels are, and the bedding. Come on, Pa. It's not good for you to sleep so little.'

'It's getting light now. And I wasn't sleeping anyway. It felt like there was a tighthead prop using my head for a ball.' He sits down and lights a cigarette. 'I came in here so that I wouldn't wake Ma.'

'I'm awake now.' Their bedroom door opens. Two corgis spill from the room, cocoon-fat, clattering on the tiles. Jonty's long ears still stand out at 90 degrees to his head, as though he's forever in a car with his head out of the window. Hansie rolls onto his back and waits for us to scratch his speckled belly. Stepping over him, Marie smokes rings around us as she hugs everyone hello. There is one wide streak of red in her hair; the rest is grey. It used to be the other way round.

'Thanks Martin, but you don't know which towels are for where, which bedding is for which room. I took it all up with us after last Christmas and washed it there, because the water here turns the sheets brown as biscuits.' She opens the door on an old wardrobe stooping in the corner of the room by the window. The ends of her hair are still tucked under her chin from a shower cap. 'Here,' she says, pulling a pile of linen from the cupboard. 'These are for you, Martin.' She makes a smaller pile. 'And these are for you, Renate.' I nod and hold the stiff sheets to my chest.

'Thanks, Ma,' my father says. 'Which room am I in?'

'You're in the middle room off the stairs.' Marie looks around for an ashtray. 'And you're in the little room under the stairs, Renate. You can't get to it from inside the house. The door is there near where you parked.' Her pack of cigarettes has her initials written on it in permanent marker. 'Pa, will you find the key for Renate?'

'It's OK,' I say. 'Don't get up. Just tell me where the key is and I'll get it.'

'Thanks, love,' he says. 'It's in the bowl in the pantry, next to the dog food.'

'Is there anything we can help with?' my father asks, opening windows. The curtains cough in the wind. 'Cleaning or shopping or something?'

'I'm telling you, Martin, Pa and I haven't had a chance to pick our noses there's been so much to do.' Her wooden bangles agree loudly. 'My back's been playing up so Pa's had to do a lot of the carrying from downstairs. The coal for barbeques and the fruit and the wine.' The room is smoke-blue. 'But we haven't had a chance to go shopping yet, and we need more water.'

'What's wrong with the water here?'

'It stains my teeth.'

I watch them from the pantry door, my foot on Hansie's belly. My father with a hand on his mother's shoulder and his father picking at his flaking fingernails. They are all older and thinner than the last time I saw them.

'OK, I'll drive into Jeffrey's later this morning, after I've had a sleep,' my father says. 'You OK to stay here, Renate?'

'Yes. Ja.' I am English now and I can tell they don't like it. They roll the r in my name and it becomes hard and forceful as a verb.

'She can come with us to walk the dogs,' Marie says.

From outside comes the sound of a helicopter. It shames the swallows with its noise. My father slides open the glass door and we stand on the patio and watch it land on the beach. Its windows blink in the sun like a bluebottle fly.

We drive down to the beach because Marie's back won't make the hill. Because Walt is too tired and Hansie too fat. I sit in the back with the dogs. The BMW's leather seats are covered in black jersey material to protect against claws and hair. Walt used to love this car; he wouldn't even smoke in it.

Marie turns to ask me questions about work and boyfriends. My answers are smooth as pebbles, tested out on friends. She laughs and asks if I have a nemesis. Maybe I learnt to ask strange questions from her somehow, but I don't know when. I choose someone and tell her about him. 'He has a face like a bird of prey that's been in one too many scrapes,' I say as we park at the gate to the beach. She laughs again.

'Who is this guy?' Walt asks.

'She just told you.'

'I was driving.'

'Oh.'

We put the dogs on their leashes. There are people on the beach now, crowding around the helicopter. Mainly fathers and their little boys. Hansie waits until we are just through the gate; his legs quiver with the effort of crouching. Marie kicks at the sand to hide it when he's done. I had expected a plastic bag. We walk down to the water, but Jonty starts to pull away at the high tide mark, so we stop, and Walt lights a cigarette. The smoke hangs in the air, a brain scan made of breath.

'Jonty's scared of the sea,' Marie says. 'It's one of the worst things I've ever heard, being scared of the sea.' She pulls at the tips of hair that have blown into her mouth. 'We're going to walk them a little way along the beach.'

'Not too far though because Hansie's too fat to walk far,' Walt says.

'He's walking further now than he used to be able to,' Marie says. She frowns at Walt and puts on her sunglasses. 'You can stay here if you want, Renate. Look at the helicopter, or for some shells we can put in the glass jars in the living room.'

I nod.

As they turn, one dog each, and start walking in the direction of the rocks, Walt says: 'They're so fat because of all that pasta you feed them. And the burgers you make for them.'

'They need the fibre, Pa.'

I can't hear them anymore, but I know the argument is scripted they've had it so often. I pull my sunglasses and my camera from my bag. In the early morning haze, the dogs are just outlines. Dog; Marie; dog; Walt. This is a good photograph. Walt is a little stooped and slower than Marie, but it's the only photo I have of them. I don't think they have any of me. If they do, it'll be from the last time I was out here from England, not from when they lived down the street from our flat and had a swimming pool and a garden and tinned pineapples. All the things I used to imagine.

Up close, you can see that Walt is dying. His fingers are too swollen for his wedding ring. I saw it on the sideboard in the living room, the gold cloudy with 40 years of wear. His fingerprints have sloughed off, the tips dull and silent. He is bruised, dark as plums, where people have touched him too hard. Almost every touch is too hard it seems: a dog nosing at his ankles sends him to the next room. His arms and legs bleed and do not scab over. The drugs have changed the shape of his face.

Walt and Marie have stopped by the rocks and are watching the dogs. Walt looks as though he is held together by his clothes. I take off my sandals and stand with my feet in the water. I look out to sea, the tears pooling for a few seconds in the bottom rim of my sunglasses. The water washes the plough snails in and out.

The chokka boats are back tonight. There are eight of them, their lights bright enough to swallow all the stars. I sit on the patio with an initialled packet of cigarettes Marie gave me.

My father says chokka can change colours. They can make their top halves look muddy and brown so that tuna won't see them. But underneath: underneath oranges, greens and reds will move across them in patterns, like seismometers or cardiographs.

The helicopter has gone, but it will come back tomorrow Burt says. Tomorrow is spring tide so it will have to land on the old tennis court between trips. Fourteen men are still missing. A chokka boat sank here in the storms the day before yesterday. Three men were picked up alive, and a body washed up in Cape St Francis earlier today. The beaches have been empty, the water still too full of dead and bloated men. Tomorrow, though, it's supposed to be 35 degrees out, and the beaches will be full. The thought of dead bodies floating with outstretched hands and missing eyes will waver above the beachgoers' heads like the heat, and then dissipate.

The couple that owns the small shop that sells Cornettos and buckets and spades sent their son into Humansdorp for the early edition of the newspaper, and then again for the late one. We have one of the two. It lies on the table under a jug of water and an ashtray. We'll be able to read tide tables on the plastic top tomorrow. The paper says the coastguard has given up hope of finding anyone alive. Now, they're just looking so that the families could have some closure.

Earlier, we'd talked about what it would be like to find a body in the dunes.

'I found a seal once,' my father said. 'I knew as soon as the smell hit me that something had died.' He was sitting by the window, which was covered in green netting to keep the sticky-backed beetles out. Bananas browned in the fruit salad on the counter.

'Last time we were here, we found a huge jellyfish on the beach,' Marie said. 'Pa turned it over so that the sea could take it back more easily and children couldn't poke it with sticks.' She lit a cigarette. 'Underneath, it looked like a kiwi fruit. It was so beautiful.'

After dinner, Marie had massaged Walt's brows and cheekbones. He closed his eyes, and from the sink where I was doing the washing-up, looked cat-happy. We didn't know it then, but his skull was being hollowed out, termite-like, by the disease.

Later, we played two rounds of poker. Marie kept forgetting the order of the hands and went all in on a pair of threes. She told the story of how her grandfather had fed her her own chicken when she was young, and how he'd seen the sea once and been unimpressed by how small it was.

It's cold out on the patio and noisy with insects. I pull my legs under me and put my hands in my jersey. I've been here once at spring tide before. The water came all the way to the gate and joined up with the lagoon behind the dune. The beach shuddered under a coat of dirty foam like a dog in the bath. I'd gone walking with Walt and Marie. It was before he was sick. Before I was English and they were Walt and Marie. Then, they were Ouma and Oupa. Our calves had been scummed black, and I'd stubbed my toe on a rock I hadn't seen through the foam.

If the tide isn't too high tomorrow, I'll walk to the Point in the soft dunes. I'll go early, before I can burn, and follow the secret trails where the seagulls have oared across the sand. At the Point, I'll look for anemones in rockpools, and if there is a man there, bloated and coming off his bones, the colour beaten out of his overalls by the waves and the rocks, his mouth full of salt and his fingers nicked and nibbled at, I will push him back into the water with my foot and watch the sea take him back, take him away.

Rachel Sargeant

Rachel Sargeant grew up in Lincolnshire and studied German and Librarianship at University College Wales in Aberystwyth. A career in libraries in the south east of England followed before a move to Germany where she retrained as a swimming teacher and a teacher of English as a second language. She still lives there with her family and teaches English to university students. Having taken up storytelling and writing when her children were small, she has told stories in schools and nurseries, and had a few short stories published. Her first novel *Long Time Waiting* is due to be published by Robert Hale Ltd in August 2010.

Born Not Made

'Go on, Mozza, chuck it, you idiot,' yelled Luke.

Hubcap in hand, Mozza was close enough to the car to be sure of smashing the glass. It was just the right type – silver paintwork that gleamed so much your acne shone back at you, starchy leather seats that looked like torture even for the fattest backside, and tinted rear windows behind which some toffee-nosed git could flick you V-signs without you knowing. The poseur who owned the car, and had been daft enough to park it round here, was begging for it. He could well afford a new windscreen, but Mozza was still hesitating, enthralled by the car's CD player that had been left on. It was giving off a sound like honey, sweet and slow that oozed into Mozza's head and trickled down to the heart. Most people would think it was a violin but Mozza knew it wasn't. Mr Leopold had explained it once in class. It was a viola.

'What you waiting for? It'll be insured. That sort always are,' said Luke.

Mozza didn't move, not wanting to break the spell and let the honey go rank.

'Just chuck it, you nutter.'

Mozza couldn't hear him. The viola was well lux. It was like being allowed to stay over at Nan's when Naomi was having one of her bad days. At Nan's there was always a soak in a proper bath before bed. Soapy and warm.

'You've bottled it, haven't you, you girl,' shouted Luke.

That did it. The warm bath turned arctic-cold. Giving it some real welly, Mozza frisbeed the hubcap through the windscreen, watched for the splintered spider's web to form around the hole, and then belted away. But as the car alarm ripped the viola music to shreds, Mozza couldn't help but slow down to listen to it. If the pitch of the screeching could be varied, the beat would be strong enough to make a decent tune. Mr Leopold had a tune with the same rhythm on his iPod. He'd passed it round class once for them all to have a listen. Some famous dead bloke had written it for flutes and trumpets and stuff.

'Leg it now,' shouted Luke again, crashing through Mozza's thoughts.

Mozza speeded up and overtook Luke as the pair nipped up the steps to the flats. Luke dived through his front door, lobbing a breathless 'See you tomorrow' over his shoulder. Mozza galloped onwards, dodging a couple of foil trays of half-finished curry that had been dumped on the concrete, and trying not to breathe in too often. The stairwell had a stink all of its own, although their bog got a bit like it, too, sometimes, when Naomi was on a bender.

Four flights up and after a hefty shove to the weather-warped front door, Mozza reached home and found Naomi picking shards of glass out of the kitchen floor. There seemed to be a new orange stain there, too, but it was hard to tell the new from the old anymore.

'It just fell,' she said and kept her head down like a toddler caught doing something naughty.

'Leave it, Mum. I'll clear it. You can get back to bed,' said Mozza.

Naomi rose unsteadily to her feet and leant back against the cooker. 'It was an accident. It could happen to anyone,' she said, wrapping her dressing gown over her tracksuit.

Even from the doorway her breath said what kind of accident. Mozza fetched the dustpan and brush.

'You're a good kid. I'm going to get you a present. Show how much I love you,' she slurred, twiddling the redundant cooker knobs. They hadn't noticed at first when the gas had been disconnected. Mozza survived mostly on pizzas out of the microwave, as Naomi wasn't much of a cook, and even less of an eater.

'There's no need for a present, Mum,' said Mozza wearily, setting about the wreckage of Naomi's cider bottle on the mottled lino.

'I mean it this time. I can get you a keyboard,' she said.

'A keyboard?' Mozza looked up again, suddenly playing the child, an excited one. 'For real? No way. Wait till I tell Luke.'

Naomi's gaze hit the dirty floor. 'You'd best not tell anyone, love.'

'Why not? Are you saying it's knock-off?'

She tried a lopsided grin. 'I won't say if you don't want me to.'

Mozza stared at her, refusing to smile back but feeling guilty when her face turned in on itself, full of hurt.

She said, 'I know it's not quite what you wanted but where would we put a blinking great piano in here? And, besides, no delivery bloke would risk a hernia to shove the blasted thing up this high even if you paid him in solid gold scratch cards. Keyboard or piano – what's the difference?'

Mozza didn't answer but pictured the piano in Mr Leopold's classroom. You had to hang around for ages waiting for the music toffs like Toni Salieri to push off so there was a chance to have a go on it alone. Mozza wanted to tell Naomi that the sounds you played on the piano didn't just move from your hand to your ear like the tones of a keyboard, they went into your belly. You kind of ate them, but slowly, like ice cream. With strawberry sauce. And sugar sprinkles. And a chocolate flake. They were real.

Naomi had stopped fiddling with the cooker and was gazing down expectantly. The hurt had gone from her eyes and been replaced by a more familiar look. Mozza called it her 'pick and mix' face. With excitement, desperation and vulnerability in equal measure, she'd used it several times to good effect when the catalogue woman came for her money. She was unleashing it on Mozza now.

'A keyboard would be great, Mum. Thanks a lot,' said Mozza and kissed her soft, booze-breathy cheek before heading for the bin with the dustpan full of glass.

'Are you coming down the arcade this dinner time?' Luke asked at school the next morning.

Mozza's heart sank. Luke could be a right wind-up merchant when he wanted. Why did he ask that same stupid question every Monday when he must have known the answer by now? Mozza swallowed hard, knowing damn well what would come next, and said, 'I've got choir practice.'

Luke grinned and took his cue. 'Singing's for saddos,' he said, pretending to retch.

'No, it's not. It's…' They didn't just sing at choir. Mr Leopold told them stuff about music. He was well sound - the only teacher allowed to use Mozza's real name and not get silently cursed to beggary and back. Choir was solid - apart from when Toni Salieri and the other singers treated Mozza like something they'd trodden in. They could make you hate the feel of your own skin sometimes, but it was worth it for Mr Leopold's music. That was all that mattered most of the time. Music took Mozza away from Mozza. When Mr Leopold played piano, you didn't just listen, you breathed it in.

Mozza looked at Luke. He was the best mate in the world, the one you wanted on your side, the one you'd fight tooth and mobile for if you had to, but some things were best left unsaid. Saying true things caused bother sometimes, and the things that caused the most bother were the truest of all.

'You're right. I only go to choir to get an early dinner pass. They're all a bunch of losers,' said Mozza, putting on a show of retching too.

'How do you stick it with those show-offs? That Toni one is so up herself 'cos she's in the choir and plays the guitar,' said Luke.

'It's a cello.'

'You what?'

'She plays the cello. It makes a rich, mellow sound.'

'Except when she's playing it.' Luke drew an imaginary cello bow across his throat and let out a painful wail. They ran off laughing as Luke continued his impression of Toni's playing into the playground.

Mr Leopold tapped his baton against the music stand and asked the choir a question, 'What note do we start on?'

Mozza's hand shot up but it was pushed aside by Toni's.

She called out, 'It's a D, Sir. I'm learning the same tune on the cello. I'll be able to perform it in assembly soon.'

Can't wait for that, thought Mozza. Did the stuck-up cow ever open her mouth without scoring a perfect ten on the Pompous Scale?

Mr L. seemed to be wondering the same thing. He thanked her for yet another of the expansive answers he'd come to expect from her and called the others to order, 'Now, everyone, after three.'

The choir came in on time, some of them hitting the note more accurately than others. The music bubbled joyously inside Mozza's chest. Mr Leopold always picked good songs for them to try. This one was beautiful – apart from the middle, which was too 'samey' for Mozza's liking. It got like that with tunes sometimes. It was the same with teachers. They started off all smiles and full of promise at the beginning of term, but then they'd rumble on for weeks in a colourless routine. There'd be a flurry of excitement the first time they shouted their faces off at Luke and sent him out, but even that became predictable after a while. And as for the detention slips they doled out, they got like confetti at a cheap wedding: a lark at the time but a beggar to clear up afterwards. Why couldn't teachers – and tunes – perk up before they reached the home straight? It was all very well handing out chocky bars and quiz sheets in the last week, but what about chucking in a few mid-term videos and a hotdog? All Mr Leopold's song needed was a change of pace in the middle with a few more highs and it would be a cracking melody.

Mr Leopold put down his baton and the choir dribbled to a halt. He looked at Mozza. 'Was that a descant you had going there? You sang eight bars of notes I've never heard before.'

'Mozza's tone deaf, Sir. Didn't you know?' sneered Toni. Most of the others sneered along with her. Mozza was a joke specially arranged for their amusement.

Mozza, ready to rearrange Toni's vocal chords, but managing to keep calm in front of Mr Leopold, said, 'I thought it sounded better with a what-d'ya-call-it, a key change.'

Toni and her entourage sniggered but Mr Leopold told them to shut up and tossed Mozza a hearty thumbs-up. 'I think the idea has some merit – good thinking – but for now let's all stick to what the composer intended. Like this …' He took a deep breath and demonstrated what he meant.

'Tone deaf, tone deaf,' chanted Toni in Mozza's ear under the cover of Mr Leopold's singing. She was silenced when Mozza's fist connected with her jaw.

At home time, Mozza's pocket contained another detention slip.

Luke offered his words of comfort. 'I don't know what you're so steamed up about. Your mum never reads them.'

'I'm banned from choir for a month. It wasn't my fault. She asked for it. You'd think I'd smashed her teeth in with all the fuss she made. When I see Toni Salieri again, she's dead meat.'

Luke pointed across the school field. 'Now's your chance.'

There was no mistaking Toni's confident gait despite the weight of the cello case on her back. She looked like an arrogant black tortoise. 'Get her,' they screamed together and hurled themselves over the field. They were on her before she saw the danger. Luke yanked off the cello and Mozza grappled her to the ground but she fought back, pulling Mozza's hair. They rolled back and forth across the grass.

Luke took the cello from its case and brought it up over his head, ready to smash it down. 'Hey, Mozza, watch this.'

'No.' Mozza let go of Toni and caught the cello, knocking Luke over. 'You can't do that. Don't break it. It's…'

Luke stood up, rubbing a bruised elbow. He stared at Mozza. It was his special face: both dead hard and deadpan at the same time. He pulled it whenever the other kids laid too far into Mozza. They'd see Luke's face and scarper but it had never been turned on Mozza before. Mozza laid the cello in the case and wanted to climb in after it and shut the lid. 'We're alright, aren't we… mate? Say something, please.'

'You've gone soft,' said Luke eventually. He sloped away, ignoring Mozza's attempts to apologise.

Mozza was about to go after him when Toni saw her chance and went for a dead-leg, giving Mozza just enough time to grab her sweatshirt and take her down too. The punches were for Luke now. He wasn't mates anymore because of her.

But the revenge was short-lived. A familiar baritone voice boomed over them, 'You two, my office now.'

'Just as well you saved my cello,' mocked Toni when Mr Leopold left them alone in the music room to cool off. 'You can't get musical instruments on credit in your Mum's crummy catalogue and she can't nick 'em from Aldi neither.'

Fury – white hot and burning – spiralled upwards. Mozza's insides were going to melt if the rage didn't find an outlet, preferably against Toni's backside. No one disrespected Naomi and kept the use of their legs. She was Mum. She did her best. In her way.

Toni sauntered over to Mr Leopold's piano and lifted the lid. Only the risk of missing the target and kicking the piano instead, together with the thought of the ensuing permanent choir ban, kept Mozza's boots away from Toni's kidneys.

She played the opening bars of something Mozza didn't recognise. It wasn't a bad tune although it hardly flowed under her fingership. It needed more life. It was like Luke, boring and bad-tempered, when the neighbour's dog had kept him awake all night.

'That's not music. It's a virus. I'd call it audio dog mess that clings to your ear and you can't scrape it off.'

Toni stood up. 'Go on then, if you think you can do better.'

Mozza looked at the piano keys. Whenever Mr Leopold played, his hands slid effortlessly back and forth as if stroking a velvet blanket. He'd taught the class how each note sounded and showed them where to find middle C. When you sneaked a go after choir, you could imagine it sounded the same, but it was different now with Toni watching. 'We're not supposed to touch…'

'You can't play, can you? Not a single note,' sneered Toni, folding her arms.

No way was Mozza giving her the satisfaction. With fingers like soggy chips, Mozza sat down at the piano stool and attempted the same notes Toni had played. It sounded rubbish, like trying to run across the footie pitch, pinched into last year's trainers. But only a wimp would back out now without wiping the smug grin off Toni's face. Mozza kept on going, repeating the piece again and again, blocking out the sound of Toni cackling gleefully whenever she heard a mis-keyed note. Eventually the music took on a life of its own. The velvet that Mr Leopold caressed when he played was at Mozza's fingertips. But it didn't stop there. It coursed up Mozza's arms, flowing into the chest, belly, head, everywhere. Mozza wasn't in detention anymore, but living, out of this world. The melody made Mozza think of Luke – thundering up school corridors, offering two fingers to the "Don't Run" signs; pinging bits of rubber at the front row in registration; being Mozza's friend when everyone else called out 'weirdo.'

'It's supposed to be in C minor,' said Mr Leopold, suddenly reappearing.

Mozza's fingers froze and then banged off the edge of the keys. It wouldn't be just a choir ban this time. Mozza was buried.

Toni started yapping, 'Mozza called your tune a virus, Sir.'

Mr Leopold ignored her. 'Let me hear you play that again, properly,' he said.

Mozza shuffled awkwardly on the stool. Play it Mr Leopold's way and maybe there'd be a chance of getting back in the choir, but the music didn't taste right. Something had to be said. 'I could begin in C minor but the other one – er – C major sounds happier, like someone ducking and weaving - having a laugh. Like this, Sir.' Mozza's hands set to work, creating the melody as they glided.

Mr Leopold listened mesmerised. 'Have you composed anything else?' he asked.

'Compose? Me?' Was he having a laugh? Posh people did composing. And yet the piano did seem even better when you played your own stuff. 'Do you think Luke would like it? Can I play it for him just once? Before you ban me forever, like.'

'If you play it for me first,' said Mr Leopold.

Mozza started hesitantly. Was Mr L. for real, or was this some sick nightmare, some make-believe fairytale that would end in waking up in the flat with Naomi cider-snoring close by? Then Luke's ice-cold angry face crossed into Mozza's mind. That definitely hadn't been a dream. Mozza wanted rid of the ugly memory and whipped up the music to recall the good times, like when Luke freewheeled across the sports hall on the library trolley and crashed into the Year Ten gym mats. Higher and higher Mozza played, beating, stirring, rousing, falling to low E and climbing back up again before crashing to an end with a thunderous set of chords.

It took Mr Leopold sometime to catch his breath. When he could speak again, he said, 'Well, Wendy Mozzard, what are we going to do with talent like yours, young lady?'

Yana Stajno

Yana Stajno was born in Zimbabwe of Polish and French parents, and went to Cape Town University where she was active in guerrilla theatre. She's lived in London since the seventies where she practises as an acupuncturist. On discovering the healing effect of stories on her patients, she's developed a passion for writing and painting narratives. She's written plays for radio and stage, has had a short story published in a Serpent's Tail anthology, and has completed a Certificate in Novel Writing at City University. *Timeshare*, a first novel, is short-listed in the *Bridge House Publishing Debut Novel* competition.

Ten Plastic Roses

It was a Monday in August - brilliant sunshine, warm, hot, even. The dogs were panting in the back of the Fiat Uno I was trying to park into too small a space.

This was the day (thirteen years, nine months and six days after I should have done, I grant you) that I had banished Richard from my heart, mantelpiece and my life.

I had thrown out his bouquet.

My neighbours' terraced houses were blameless, with their colour-glossed doors and tightly snipped hedges. As I coaxed Billy and Tina back to my own more exuberant garden, I could see from the opened lids, that all the other houses' wheelie bins were empty.

But there, on the pristine pavement, leaning against my fern-crested wall, black, shining, and bulging, was the refuse bag containing his last gift to me. The plastic bag had been opened clearly, checked even, and then left outside my wheelie bin, uncollected. That the Council should take it upon themselves to reject that distasteful remnant of Richard was unthinkable. I had to get to the bottom of it.

Disappearing round the corner was the Council's rubbish truck.

I reversed the dogs to the car, heaved them into the boot, started the engine and drove, full speed, towards the truck.

A worker in a balaclava was emptying a bin with a ferocity that sent a tomato can coursing down the pavement in a wild clanging dance. He gave it an angry look. I stopped the car between the can and his stare.

'Excuse me, but you've forgotten to take my rubbish.'

Ignoring me, he descended on the next bin.

'Is there a reason?' I persisted.

He aimed, kicked this bag towards the van, like a footballer.

A flash of plastic. A metal crunch. A gap between his teeth appeared.

'Right!' I said.

I've never been good at parking. It was something that drove Richard to despair and into the arms of that ghastly driving instructor woman. I went into reverse, then forwards, with a grinding of gears. The dogs growled as I emerged from the car, armed with pen and notebook.

'Your name, please.'

Two other workers appeared.

'Which of you is the boss?'

They stared at me as if I was speaking in an ancient tongue, then shrugged.

'I'm taking down your plate number of your cab' - I tapped my notebook - 'a description of each of you, and -'

I ran after them, but running, shouting, and trying to take notes simultaneously isn't easy.

We were all out of breath. No, I was out of breath. The first man was emerging from his balaclava.

I have the notes. The writing plunges from top left to bottom right with some seriously wavy graphs mid-centre. Red beard, bristly red nostril hairs. There's a wild bump in the middle of the word hairs. Then it reads in huge lettering which crosses two pages, his answer: Garden refuse.

'What are you calling garden refuse? If it's a bunch of ten red roses tied with ribbon, they are artificial and indestructible.'

From the interior of his bin van, he chanted, 'If you've got those sorts of problems, phone Social Services, Madam.'

They make an amazing noise, those bin vans, when speeding. Like the end of the world.

My landline lives in my front room, on a dresser unsteady with cups, saucers, books, all my old letters and postcards. I located it under a heap of red bills and got down to business. I finally got the Chief Council Rubbish Collection Information Officer on the line. A Ms Tidewell.

'I take my olive oil bottles to the bottle bank, my Sunday supplements to the paper bank, my live yoghurt cartons to the carton bank' - I gathered breath for a fresh onslaught – 'and the only thing I expect the most overpaid local Council in the European Community to do, is to collect my unrecyclable rubbish once a week.'

Ms Tidewell - to give her her due - did her civic best.

'I can hear you're upset.'

'Upset?' I was now pacing as well as talking. 'I am not upset, my dear Ms Tidewell.' I tried to disengage myself from the telephone wire, which had wrapped itself around my jumper. 'I simply want your Council Rubbish Collection Inspector to come and tell me exactly what it is in my rubbish that the Rubbish Collection Department is objecting to. Do you understand?'

At which point my attempts to unravel the bloody-minded telephone flex led me to the window in time to see the balaclava'd rubbish collector daring to lift the contentious bag into the air.

'Hold on.' I yelled at Ms Tidewell.

I launched myself out of my front gate. 'Leave my bag alone. It's evidence, do you hear? Evidence.'

He seemed not to hear me, gazing beyond me as if I was about to be swallowed by a killer whale. I resisted the temptation to look behind for one and kept my attention pinned to a spot between his eyebrows. When I managed to harness his focus to my own, he appeared not to recognise me. It could have been the way I was hanging onto the bag so that the sharp plastic stalks of ten roses were pointing at his jugular. Or, it could have been the fact that my green wellies were clashing wildly with my lilac sundress. Or, perhaps, he heard the racket the dogs were making. But if he thought I was intimidated by his 'she-is-an-object' look, he could think again. Not me. And certainly not now.

'I want that bag vindicated, do you hear? Leave it exactly where you found it.'

He let go, walking backwards slowly, which, I thought, was overdoing it.

I stomped up the front path to find the door locked. So I had to wait for the van to clank away, before digging in under weeds for the spare key. It was rusty, but worked, luckily. In the hall, I tripped over Tina, who nipped me. Swearing, I grabbed the phone; the connection was dead.

The Council's switchboard had considerable difficulty in relocating Ms Tidewell. But I used nail clippers to fill in time. It was after the dogs and I had impeccably trimmed nails, that Ms Tidewell's thin voice reassembled itself on the line.

'Yes?'

'I want you to know that until I receive a visit from your Inspector, you are to leave my bag alone. Or else,' - I took a large gulp of air – 'you'll regret you ever heard from me.'

'Yes,' was all she said.

I didn't want those roses taken away by stealth. They needed an honourable, above-board, legitimate exit from my life. After all, from their spot on the mantelpiece, they'd surveyed the life I'd built for my son, all on my own. All afternoon I worried that the bin man would sneak away with my bag while I was at work. I was considering leaving my patients pinned to the acupuncture table to rush off to check. Somehow, I managed to resist.

When I got home the bag was still there. But I found a hole oozing lamb bone with maggots. And there was a hand-delivered envelope on the doormat.

Rubbish tipping is an offence, signed, Ruth E Tidewell.

I used the paper to reinforce the bag's maggot-infested hole and tried to get some sleep. I awoke from a nightmare - a giant crab was ripping open a human eye - to a sound I recognised - the squelch of plastic being compressed. I shoved my head out of the window, and caught a fleeting glimpse of someone running.

'Who's that?'

I threw on a t-shirt and knickers, and hared off in the direction the figure had gone. Apart from the sound of windows crashing open in the street around me, I found no other sign of life. I went back to my precious bag, to find it jumbled about, but there.

I sat at the front window, guarding, until dawn.

Now I had a real problem. I had to go to work early. I hauled my son out of his bed,

'Mummm?'

I insisted he install himself at the front window for the day.

'I want you to guard that bag.'

'Y're what?'

He was bleary-eyed.

'I'm waiting for the Council Inspector to inspect it.'

'Muuuum, I've got to go to school.'

'It's important, Simon. It's a matter of principle.'

'But, I haven't had any breakfast.'

'I'll bring you scrambled eggs on toast, and put your lunch ready in a container.'

'I gotta be here the whole day?'

'I'll pay for you.'

'Wicked. How much?'

'£20.'

'£30.'

'£25.'

'What's *in* the bag anyway?'

I went to the Garden Centre, soon as it opened.

'Chicken wire, please! Two metres, I'm in a rush.'

I unloaded it from the car. There is a satisfaction in finishing something well. My bag looked sculptural under mesh. I helped a wheelchair user around it, then went to work where my patients learnt to voice their symptoms in sound bites.

When I drew the thin thread of Ruth Tidewell's voice out of the Council's telephone switchboard, she didn't give me a moment to speak.

'We have defined your refuse as bulky,' she said. 'The next bulky rubbish collection date is the 15th of September.'

'Bulky? It is not bulky. I want my bag accepted for what it is.'

She'd gone.

I returned to my treatment room and actually told Mr X, who'd been in the same mid-life crisis for 15 years, with the same accompanying nervous cough, to just come clean and tell his wife that he was gay. I hoped he'd thank me for it one day. It was tough keeping my focus; I was relieved to be going home.

The chicken wire was intact. Glinting in the street light. Sculptural. Beautiful. Empty. My stomach gave a lurch. Downwards. I stood there, numb. Lost. I couldn't believe it. I felt like a traveller who has got to the horizon on faith, only to discover that there really is a line beyond which lies the void.

I clicked the door shut behind me very quietly and found two boys in the hall, bending over something. Why wasn't Nat at school? And, more to the point, why wasn't Simon at his handsomely paid post?

'It's been taken,' I said.

Simon was shifting his weight around, something he does when he's lying. 'Er, no, Mum, it's here.' He stood up to reveal a full bin liner.

'We thought it needed to come in,' said Nat, lip curled as if I was incompetent.

'In case it rained,' added Simon.

I looked at the bag. It was neatly tied, bulging even.

But it wasn't mine.

It didn't have a hole, or a smell, and, when I ripped it open, it was crammed full of newspapers from the recycle bin.

I didn't say anything. I just sat on the floor and put my head in my hands.

Simon was close to tears. 'Honest, Mum, we've been sitting at the window all day. Just that we were on the PlayStation and Nat was winning and next thing we looked up and - there it was - gone.'

Simon glanced at Nat, who was examining a crack in the plaster.

'Whoever took it, must have crawled,' he said.

'We tried Mum, we really did.'

I looked at Simon's puckered face. My own flesh and blood.

'What was in it, anyway?' asked Nat.

'It's alright, Simon, don't cry. Don't cry.'

I stepped into the front room. Closed the door behind me. Let silence settle into the dust of my grandmother's cups and saucers, the corners of the old letters and postcards from a forgotten time, resound into the pile of red bills. Had I gone mad? Why was refuse collecting taking possession of my mind?

I told myself to think of something else. But I couldn't stop thinking about those everlasting dusty roses, winging their way to a landfill site, and Richard, damn him.

The television went on in the kitchen, the kettle was singing, Billy's snores were wafting through the crack between my door and the carpet. Her blocked sinuses were too expensive to fix.

May Richard's perfectly pressed trousers spawn mushrooms along their creases. And with those knife edged pleats in mind, I plucked out an old address book. I flicked through it and found a faded name and phone number. Picking up the phone, I dialled a number I hadn't dialled for a long, long time.

'Richard?...Who? Why, it's Melanie. Yes, it has been a while. How many?... No, more like thirteen and a half. Fine. You're fine? Good. Very good. Busy, you know, being a Mum. Three? All with that driving instructor? Congratulations. Me? Oh, just the one. A he. Thirteen next Tuesday. Yours. No, he's your son. I didn't keep the appointment at the clinic, you see.'

It had gone silent at the other end of the phone. There was some background noise, though, of kids' voices or the television.

'But Richard, I wanted to ask you - why on earth did you send me artificial roses? Fresh ones would have been so much more...' The phone went dead. 'Bastard,' I said to no-one in particular.

Staring out at my front garden, I let the receiver drop. The jasmine and tree peonies were strangled by bindweed. The hedge was high, lumpy, unruly and cut out the light. It was time I did something about it. It was also time I burnt those old letters and paid some bills.

I opened the door, passed Simon's bag sculpture, chucked it outside the door and called out:

'Nat, Simon, what would you like for supper?'

Natasha Tripney

Natasha Tripney lives in London. She studied English Literature at King's College in London before abandoning the city briefly to complete an MA in Writing at Warwick University where she won the *Derek Walcott Prize*. She writes short stories and occasionally begins bigger things in between writing about theatre for *The Stage* and various online publications.

An Experiment

From below, the sound of voices, a dull hum. The sound floats up through the gaps between floorboards and runs right through her, from her silk-slippered feet to her fingertips. When they laugh – which they do often – it sounds like the muffled thump of drums. She stands very still and tries to picture them moving about below. First there is the particular scrape of a chair being pushed back from a table, then the streaming of wine from decanter to glass, the faint re-housing of a crystal stopper. Then a pause, then the clink-clink-clink of a toast. They are in good spirits. A humorous thing must have been said for the drums boom once more. Something of their laugh slips into her and she finds herself smiling with them. She makes a noise, a little ripple of amusement, which sounds such an odd, echoing note in the empty room, she immediately wishes she could take it back.

She turns her attention to the window. Outside the sky is empty of cloud, an impenetrable greyish-white. It seems to her as if the world beyond the far hedgerow is unfinished, as if it simply runs out into nothing. She has been watching the spider for a while. It sits in the corner of the bottommost pane, trembling on its web. She taps the glass with her nail and wonders if it sees her, whether it is studying her as she is studying it. She has an enquiring mind or so she has been told. That is one of the things Mr Harding most admired in her; that is one of the main reasons she was brought here.

She hears the creak of the stair banister, followed by the dormouse scamper of Mrs Thwaite, ascending. She chooses to remain by the window. Mrs Thwaite knocks lightly on the door and enters before any reply can be made, as is her way.

'Cecily,' she says, voice tinged with reprove.

Mrs Thwaite is a thin, straight-spined woman of nearly fifty years; there are no bends in her, or at least there do not seem to be, her body is a collection of black lines. 'Cecily', she repeats with a softer tongue, 'they are asking to see you now. It is time.'

Mrs Thwaite crosses the room and begins to fiddle with Cecily's dress, finding all manner of small faults in need of correction: a bunching of lace at the neck, a ribbon askew, a rumpled sleeve in need of smoothing. The weight of the fabric still feels alien to Cecily; she lifts an arm and allows the heavy cream silk to shift in ripples across her skin. Mrs Thwaite clucks and takes hold of Cecily's wrist, lowers it, just as if Cecily were a doll. 'There,' she says, satisfied. 'You look quite the picture.'

Cecily is minded to ask 'of what?' but holds her tongue and nods her head with what she hopes is the right degree of gratitude. 'How many of them are there?' she asks.

'Just five today,' Mrs Thwaite replies. 'Mr Brooks is delayed.'

Cecily relinquishes her spot by the window and follows Mrs Thwaite out of the room. She walks carefully, mindful of the cracks between the boards. She has the idea that if she were to tread on one, this new world of hers might shatter, might split, and she would tumble through the gaps, back to the place she was before she was plucked, before he came for her. She catches a glimpse of her reflection in the looking glass by the door. Seed pearl earrings bounce beneath her lobes and her hair sits in ringlets around her face. It is not an unpleasing sight but nor does she see herself in it. She struggles to connect that face, that girl, with her hot-running blood, her skin, her soul.

Downstairs they will have lunched already – the house smells of ham and suet – but they will still be, in their own way, hungry, for they come here for sustenance of both mind and body. They will, she thinks, be sitting round the large oval dining table with their cheeks pinked by the claret, their voices loud, the room aglow. Perhaps there will be some new contraption to examine or a pamphlet to dissect; they like to get a thing between their teeth, they like a project, they like a campaign.

As Cecily follows Mrs Thwaite down the stairs she tries to run through her recent French lessons in her head, to sound out the vowels in her mind; she has not thought of her French since the tutor last visited and worries that many of the new words have leaked away. As they reach the foot of the stairs the parlour door opens and the kitchen maid emerges with a tray on which some empty dishes are piled. Seeing Cecily standing there, the girl starts and dips her head respectfully, a gesture she finds herself mirroring, feeling awkward and suddenly at sea; she steps backwards and almost upsets a blue Jasper vase. A curse escapes her lips causing Mrs Thwaite's shoulders to shudder slightly. The older woman turns and fixes her with a stern, grey gaze, shaking her head and, almost tenderly, raising a hand to Cecily's face to tuck away one last, disobedient curl.

'Are you ready?' she asks.

Cecily is not sure, but she nods readily as there is no alternative gesture she can make.

Mrs Thwaite raps cautiously on the parlour door. On this occasion she waits for a reply, which takes its time in coming. 'Enter.'

As the door is opened, Cecily hears them clapping their hands in anticipation. Inside, the men are seated round the table, just as she pictured them to be, except that the tall one, Mr Cox, is standing, with his hands resting on the chair back of Mr Bolt, his wig slightly pitched to one side. On the table there are the usual array of papers and, today, a wooden display case holding plant specimens. The men all turn to face her, waiting for Mr Harding to speak first. He stands and approaches her; slight of frame and measured of manner, in no hurry. Mr Bolt and Mr Cross also stand but do not move, while the amiable Mr Gardner places both his palms on the tabletop and seems to contemplate manoeuvring the cannonball of his belly upwards, only to think better of it at the last minute. 'My dear girl,' he says warmly in compensation, the first to address her. 'Welcome, welcome.'

Mr Harding's mouth has stretched into his best attempt at a smile; he bids her to come further into the room, to not dawdle in the doorway. Cecily looks at Mrs Thwaite for reassurance, but the older woman has become stone and is standing in the corner with lowered eyes and her head bowed.

'Well,' Mr Harding said, circling her, taking in her dress, her hair, her posture, 'how are you today?' The question sounds innocent, causal, but she wonders if some trap lies within it, if her answer may in some way displease him as so often happened.

'I am quite well,' she attempts.

'Good,' he says, directing his pleasure not at her but back at his small audience around the dining table, 'I am glad to hear that. And how are your lessons progressing?'

Cecily looks from face to face. 'I am enjoying them greatly,' she says tentatively.

Mr Gardner gives a little laugh. 'Come, come, child. Are you really enjoying all your lessons equally? Your Latin grammar? Your arithmetic? You must have your favourites must you not? There must be certain things that fire your mind more than others and some subjects that must make you grit your teeth in frustration. Do not feel you have to act some role in front of us.'

Cecily feels hot under her layers of silk and taffeta. Though she feels more able to speak freely to Mr Gardner than the others, she remains wary. 'Well, I have very much enjoyed your talks on botany, Sir, and I was most excited to learn the workings of Mr Cross' coin press.'

Mr Harding flicks the air with a dismissive wave. 'You misunderstand. We are talking of your formal education, of your tutors. I have acquired the best French master north of London; surely his teaching has proven stimulating?'

'Pish,' interrupts Mr Gardner, neglecting to excuse himself despite the presence of ladies. 'Who are you to decide what constitutes a suitable education? If the girl wishes to know more about the majesty of nature, we should feed that desire. We are progressive people, are we not? Why stymie the female brain?' He speaks with evident passion and the crockery jigs a little on the table. Mr Bolt reaches protectively for his wine glass.

Mr Harding seems too busy excising something from under his

fingernail. 'Thank you Samuel,' he says in an offhand manner. 'I shall bear that in mind.' Cecily cannot quite determine whether he is amused or annoyed. In all the weeks she's been here she has still not managed to successfully gauge his moods, to understand what drives him. He can be kind, so very attentive, and he's given her so much, but he remains closed off, a puzzle. Sometimes his temper rears up like an unbroken horse, hooves flailing, and Mrs Thwaite is required to escort her from the room. Cecily is not easily upset – she'd encountered far worse at the orphanage – but she was keen to avoid such scenes. She knows that her continued presence in his home is predicated on her pleasing him, but it is proving to be a complex task.

She realises that Mr Harding is speaking to her – at her – in a swift, stream of French. She latches on to the words that she recognises and tries to formulate what she hopes is an adequate response. She has learned that a brief, demure reply is always better received than any of her more ambitious, error-flecked constructions, and this is what she delivers. Mr Harding listens and nods in satisfaction before turning back to the table, his arms aloft, inviting comment. 'There has been some excellent progress made, I'm sure you agree?'

'Oh yes,' cries Mr Bolt, perhaps more loudly than he had meant to, 'Excellent progress.'

Mr Cross simply stares at her as if she were one of the trilobites of which he is so fond, with a clinical, collector's gaze.

Mr Gardner looks at her with an air of contemplation; he seems on the verge of saying something more but instead he shrugs and enquires about the whereabouts of pudding. Mr Harding has already returned to his seat and is sorting through the mess of papers on the table. He finds the thing he is searching for and begins to show it to Mr Cross. Cecily realises she is no longer required to be here; they have moved on. Mr Harding asks Mrs Thwaite to go and see about the delayed plum duff and she departs, leaving Cicely standing on the rug. She is not sure whether to follow Mrs Thwaite or stay where she is, since she has not been officially dismissed. She decides to stay as she is enjoying being in a room that is usually off limits. The gentlemen are now debating some aspect of canal construction. Cecily listens for a while before letting her gaze drift across the walls, over the framed plans for Mr Harding's mill, immaculately inked, and the turquoise-winged butterflies pinned and mounted under glass. She is drawn to the bookcase and stands in front of the rows of leather spines, drinking in titles, some familiar, others not. She lifts out a thick, blue-boarded volume by Linnaeus and enjoys its satisfying weight in her hands. She opens its pages and studies some of the lists and tables within, trying to piece together their meaning, tracing the intricate diagrams with the tips of her fingers. She returns it to its place on the shelf and pulls out a thinner book, much-handled. She recognises the loops and curves of Mr Harding's fine handwriting on the first pages; these, she realises, are records of his own making, figures and sketches and notes. She turns over a few pages and finds her own name there, once, twice, a dozen times, in amongst the names of many other girls. Height, weight and other distinguishing characteristics are all listed alongside some comments on personality type. She is just able to read that she "shows potential" on the date of his last visit to the orphanage, before Mr Harding is at her elbow, closing the book. 'Cecily, please, we're busy here. When Mrs Thwaite returns you can go and practice your piano.' He removes the book from her hands and turns his back on her.

Mrs Thwaite seems to be as enamoured with Cecily's piano playing as Cecily is; which is to say that neither of them enjoyed the process very much. So after a few brief scales and a clipped and muddled run at some Bach, the older woman, who is sitting with her mending basket, gives Cecily her unvoiced permission to stop. Cecily springs from the piano as if she's been shackled there for hours, rather than tapping away for a mere twenty minutes, and rustles over to the window. Mr Bolt and Mr Cross are departing by carriage and from the length and volume of their farewells it appears that more claret has been consumed with pudding, or possibly some port.

There is a lumbering sound in the hall and a polite tap-tap on the doorpost. Mr Gardner looks into the room causing Mrs Thwaite to pause in her stitching. Her face wears an expression of concern and enquiry for Mr Gardner does not ascend the stairs without good reason. Without being bidden, he arranges himself on the chaise and pats at his forehead with a handkerchief.

'Cecily, child, I meant to speak to you earlier but became distracted by Cross and his bothersome canals. Honestly, the man wouldn't bend in a gale.'

Cecily is unsure how to respond so she smiles in what she hopes is an adequate manner. 'I have something for you,' Mr Gardner continues and he pulls a small, flat parcel from his pocket.

Cecily looks at Mrs Thwaite, who nods, permitting her to accept the gift. She takes the package, which is sheathed in brown paper and much wound about with string; it takes her a while to negotiate Mr Gardener's unorthodox knots, but eventually she succeeds. 'That is as good a primer on botanical matters as I've come across,' he says. 'I think you will find it very instructive.'

'Thank you,' blushes Cecily.

'There is something of the spark in you, my girl,' he says, 'and I would hate to see it go unfed. Oh, I know Harding is seeing to your material needs. The clothes, the hair; it is quite the transformation – he is most happy. And I know he is attending to your education and is most satisfied with your progress.'

Mr Gardner pauses in mid-flow. He casts a glance up at Cecily, in her layers of silk and ribbons, and his pink fingers dance across his knee. A long, slow sigh escapes his lips. 'Mr Harding has been a good friend to me over the years,' he says, parcelling out the words. 'He has a fine, questing mind, though I'll admit he sometimes takes things too far for my liking and he does not perceive the barriers that other men might. But this is what makes him the man he is and I am sure he will take very good care of you. Yes, I am sure.'

Cecily's features remain static, her mouth a girlish curl. Across the room Mrs Thwaite sits spidered over her sewing basket, offering no guidance. Mr Gardner appeared to want to give her something greater than a book of botany, she understands this much, and she wishes it was permissible to crouch by the man's side and clasp his hand and thank him. She wants to tell him that though she may be clay, a thing to be moulded, she is not without sense. She can still remember the warmth of being chosen, the feeling she felt when the stern-lipped man selected her as if he were buying a bolt of fabric. It is not the life she would have chosen but it has chosen her and she is happy with that, she must be. There have been others, she knows, who have been here before her, in these rooms, maybe even in these clothes, sized up, assessed and found wanting. She will not be one of them.

She does not bend; she remains upright and thanks Mr Gardner again for his gift. She makes him stand. With some effort he gets to his feet and bids her a hesitant farewell, before expressing some concern that he may have overindulged at lunch. As he leaves Mrs Thwaite finally folds away her sewing, but does not speak.

Still clutching her book, Cecily returns to the window and, after a while, she sees Mr Gardner emerge from the house with Mr Harding at his side. The men exchange their goodbyes as the footman gamely assists Mr Gardner into his carriage. Mr Harding watches him drive towards the gates before hurling a few sharp words at the groundsman's boy and turning back towards the now quiet house. There is no one left now, except for Mrs Thwaite, and she will want to turn in soon. Mr Harding looks up and his eyes meet Cecily's. He nods in her direction, a curt gesture, and is gone.

Cecily perches on the window seat and watches the birds curve and circle over the far meadow. She will stay here until he comes for her, she thinks, still as the millpond and striking as a butterfly under glass.

Sherri Turner

Sherri Turner was brought up in Cornwall and now lives in Surrey with her husband. She has had numerous short stories published in women's magazines in the UK and abroad and was the winner of the *Woman's Own Short Story Competition* in 2005. Sherri has been placed or short-listed in competitions for both poetry and short stories, including a commendation in the *Yeovil Prize* in 2009. She has recently been published in the charity anthology *100 Stories for Haiti* and her work will appear in two Bridge House anthologies this summer.

Being Mother

I have always thought it important to make the effort. The children appreciate it; I know they do, despite what people may think. So I've laid out the best tea-set in the garden and we will sit down properly, as a family.

It's a shame that Jimmy won't be here. He thinks it all quite absurd and prefers football. Never mind. We can't all have the same standards, can we?

The tea-set has six cups and saucers with matching tea-plates, a pot, sugar bowl and cream jug. A pattern of pretty summer flowers in pink and lavender wraps around the rim of each cup and the leaves spill over onto the handle. The children aren't old enough for tea yet, so the pot is filled with juice. It doesn't matter. It's the ceremony that's significant, doing things together, doing them right. We have biscuits, too, custard creams and chocolate chip cookies arranged in a neat spiral on one of the tea-plates. There are only five of us, so there's a plate to spare. I wouldn't like to use one that didn't match. That would spoil everything.

Emily is looking particularly lovely today. She has on her blue dress, the one with the lace collar and satin tie around the waist. I suppose it is a little old fashioned, but it suits her and she has matching ribbons tying her hair into bunches. Jimmy says she looks ridiculous in it, that girls don't wear that kind of thing today. We don't listen, Emily and I. What do men know about fashion, after all?

'Shall I be Mother?' I ask, as usual.

Nobody objects so I pour Emily's "tea" and put a biscuit on her plate and she waits politely for the others to be served. She's a real credit to me, that one.

Edward is a little grumpy, I think. He's refusing to sit up straight and his tie is askew. I have to warn him that he won't get a biscuit if he doesn't behave. It makes no difference, so I decide to serve him last. I don't really have the heart to refuse him his cookie, but it won't hurt him to wait and wonder. Discipline is so important in children, don't you think? Jimmy says I'm too strict with them. He thinks they should be allowed to play more and get dirty. All very well, I say to him, if you're going to clean them up afterwards, bathe them, wash and mend their clothes. He isn't going to, of course, so that usually shuts him up.

I move on to Christabel. She's the smallest, still a baby, though only just. I've filled the jug with milk for her, as I don't want juice to rot her teeth before they're even through. I'll have to hold the cup for her, too. I do so hate those plastic mugs with the little spout that children always seem to use these days. You have to admit they're rather common and the colours are so garish – turquoise and yellow and tangerine. I've given her a plate even though she won't be having a biscuit. Mothers these days treat all their children like babies and then they're surprised when they never grow up. There's no harm in getting them used to the real world as soon as possible and grown ups don't drink out of turquoise cups with lids.

Peter is the most mischievous. Today, though, he's sitting quietly waiting his turn. It's good to see that my parenting methods are getting through to him at last. I blame Jimmy for the way Peter can be. He's Jimmy's favourite, which is wrong and I've told Jimmy so. All the children must be treated the same, even though some personalities may be more appealing than others. Just because Peter is a little more playful, more fun Jimmy says, that doesn't excuse the fact that Jimmy virtually ignores the others. You have to look for the good in all your children and, with my four, it isn't hard to find.

Emily's the pretty one, Edward is the studious one, Christabel's the baby and Peter's the jolly one. A fine collection, if you ask me.

I serve myself last. I'm not that fond of tea, if I'm honest, and anyway there is only one pot so I have juice with the children. I allow myself two biscuits, one of each, to demonstrate the fact that there are privileges to being the mother. The children don't rule the roost in my house, as you will have noticed. I don't let the side down, though. I am also wearing a summery dress, though not as girlish as Emily's. It has a floral print, a little like the patterns on the cups and in the same colours. Attention to detail is another lesson best learned early. I did consider ribbons, but Jimmy laughed at me last time so I just brushed my hair over my shoulders. The sun glints off the pale barley colour of it and I know my children must look at me and be proud to have such a beautiful mother.

My mother has never given me that chance, the opportunity to be proud of her. I suppose it would be unfair to call her a bad mother. No doubt she does her best. There's no tea in the garden with her, though. Her favourite drink is one served in a glass and she isn't that fussy on the variety. When other mothers were making breakfast for their children or sending them off to school mine would be leaning against the kitchen sink in her dressing gown telling me that Mummy wasn't very well today and would I mind getting myself some toast.

If I was lucky she would be dressed by the time I got home. A t-shirt and some jeans would be usual, clean sometimes, more often yesterday's, picked up from the floor because the washing hadn't been done. I longed to see her in a cotton frock, her hair combed, a teacup in her hands. I wouldn't even have minded about having toast again for supper. It was the lack of standards. I knew then that I would never be that kind of mother, an embarrassment to my children, and I haven't been. It is possible to break the cycle, to create a world of calm and principles where children can learn and grow and become good citizens. I have done that and will continue to do so. I haven't seen my mother for a long time.

I finish my custard cream and juice and feel a few spots of rain. I don't want the children catching cold so I start to tidy away the tea things to take them inside. The children don't have very big appetites, although I do try to find things they like, so I eat the biscuits and drain their cups before stacking the crockery and placing it back on the tray.

I sit Edward and Peter next to the tea pot and tuck Christabel under my right arm and Emily under my left. It's a little awkward, but they don't complain. When I get back to my room I will line them up on the bed in their usual places and then wash the tea things before reading them a story. They are such good children and I know I am lucky. I do like to think that I have something to do with it, though, being the kind of mother that I am.

I cross the lawn, on my way back to the house, and almost drop the tray in shock. There is a woman walking towards me and she is calling to me. I don't get many visitors and at first I think that I am seeing things. The woman has brown hair, tied roughly back from her face, and is wearing jeans. She draws closer and I can tell that it is my mother. Although I don't really want to see her, not after all this time, I mustn't lose my manners in front of the children. Mother has another woman with her and they are talking. I can't quite hear what they are saying, something about me doing it again, and Mother has a frown on her face.

'Where have you been?' I ask, as politely as I can manage.

'I had to go home,' she says. 'You know that.'

'But I haven't seen you in ages.'

'I was here yesterday. You've forgotten again.'

I don't want to argue with her. It must be the drink, making her think things that aren't true. I try to sniff her breath and she recoils from me.

'Have you seen Jimmy?' I ask.

The other lady, the one in the white dress, looks at Mother and asks her who Jimmy is. Well, there's no reason why she should know. I've never seen her before, although she looks a bit smart to be a friend of my mother's.

'I don't really know,' Mother says to her. 'She started talking about him a few months ago. One of her friends from way back, I think.'

'Honestly,' I say, unable to contain my exasperation. 'You know Jimmy. He lives next door. He's always round here.'

She shrugs and the smart lady smiles kindly.

'Shall I take that off you, Mrs King? We don't want you having an accident, do we?'

Mrs King? Who on earth is she talking to?

'I'm sorry,' I say. 'I think you must be confused. My name is Barbara and I'm perfectly capable of carrying a tray and looking after my children.'

Mother sighs. 'Don't you think you're a bit old to be playing with dolls, Mum?'

Mum?

She tries to take Emily and I cry out.

'No! Leave her! You leave my Emily alone!'

I know the children will be shocked, but this is no time for manners. I can't let my mother take them, I can't. She's tried before, I remember now, her and the other woman. I drop the tray and gather up my children and try to get away. I'm not quick enough and Mother grabs my arm.

'Come on, Mum,' she says. 'You know they're only dolls. I'm your real daughter. Don't you remember? I'm Alice.'

I start to tremble and the other lady shakes her head and removes Mother's hand from my arm.

'Best not,' she says. 'We've tried, really we have.'

'It can't be good for her,' Mother says, as if she would have any idea of what was.

'At least she's happy,' the other woman says.

'Well, I was,' I say, 'before you came and spoiled my lovely party. What will the children think? They don't need a grandmother like you. I don't need you. Go away.'

I can see that I have made Mother cry and I'm sorry for that, truly I am. But it's a mother's job to protect her children no matter what and as I hug them in my arms I know that they will never feel about me the way I feel about my mother.

Mother kisses me on the cheek and says that she will see me tomorrow, then walks back up the lawn. The nice lady thinks I may be a little tired after all the excitement and suggests that I go for a lie down. I think that's a good idea. It has been a rather stressful day.

We head for the house, my children and I, just as the sun comes out from behind a cloud.

'Oh, look,' I say to them. 'It's brightening up a bit. Maybe we can come out for some tea after our naps. What do you think? Shall I be Mother?'

Ben Walker

Ben Walker is a gardener from Linthwaite in West Yorkshire. He began writing surreal histories in 2005. In his spare time he designs games and crosswords, and has spent a lot of time working out a system for a non-linear novel. After graduating, he volunteered on organic farms in the Pyrenees before moving to Bristol. Recently he has been working on the herbaceous border at Bristol Zoo. In the future he hopes to work with mazes on historical gardens. This is his first published story.

Bitter Gourd Fruit

Eventually I discovered I had been reincarnated as a severed head stowed in a hardwood casket aboard a ship, with all my capacity for thought, sensation and speech somehow preserved. But on first waking in the dark, I had imagined for a long time I could still feel my body beneath me. Naturally I was distressed to find any movement impossible below the neck. My guess was that the nerves in my spine had somehow been severed. On the plus side, I reasoned, my brain seemed unharmed. If I experienced a little discomfort, the general effect was no worse than a mild hangover.

After a few days' effort my eyes managed to strain a weak light through imperfections in the casket's joinery, nothing useful, but a haze without contents. Only my ears kept me amused. I knew that, after prolonged periods of sensory deprivation, fluids in the vestibular canals could sometimes begin sending faulty signals to the brain. So I wasn't surprised to be visited by impressions of movement, rocking and rising, pitching and yawing, accompanied by fragments of conversation and violin. I even began to look forward to my hallucinations. In fact, I would soon learn, my experiences were all perfectly genuine accounts of my casket's being transported through the ship below decks. In the same way, I later interpreted the opening of my casket as another delusion. Rather kindly, the ship's captain had draped a thin cloth over the hinge door so that, as he swung it open, my eyes wouldn't be overwhelmed. A pale orange glow appeared and the captain addressed me, asking if I felt comfortable. He warned he was about to remove the cloth. I explained I had been born with glaucoma, that my lenses had been surgically removed, and asked him if he would mind leaving the cloth in place. He then brought his head under the cover so it seemed we were sharing a tent. His hand appeared with a basin of water and a loofah sponge. My face was wiped and tongue wetted. He popped a number of cloves behind my gums, asking if it would be alright for him to ask me some questions. Did I know a good cure for scurvy? 'Vitamin C' I mumbled, pleased to be able to respond so brightly. He frowned. And where could that be found? 'In fruit. Lemons and limes' I replied, my tongue numbed by the cloves. 'And fresh meat?' he asked. 'No. Only in citrus fruit.' The captain nodded. 'And how does one go about calculating the longitude?'

I was taken to Captain Gray's cabin each day before dawn to discuss science and seamanship. From Gray I learned our vessel was called the Alpaca, a Bristol-built steamer. She was driven by a single screw propeller at a speed of 10 knots, had five schooner-rigged and one square-rigged mast, her length being 322 feet, her beam 50 feet 6 inches, and draught 16 feet. The crew were 75 strong. Below Captain Gray were a first, second and third mate, a boatswain and deck cadets, then the able and ordinary seamen, plus carpenters, stokers, a doctor, a navigator, two cooks, a pumpman, a priest, an oiler, a wiper, an engineer and the engineering cadet. From me Captain Gray expected a steady supply of information. Although he was more than competent in technical matters pertaining to sailing, Captain Gray's grasp of the natural world, and even his general knowledge were exceptionally poor, and I put this down to a life spent at sea. Gray was born aboard the Alpaca and he told me he never intended to set foot off her. Late one evening, as we were drinking hot chocolate together on the weather deck (mine taken through a straw) he confided that he loved every inch of his ship. I occasionally saw him stroking some part of her, a door handle or one of the windlasses.

Let it be understood that I was far from an expert in scientific matters myself. I had schooling only up to my O levels, and besides that nothing more than a curious layman's appreciation of chemistry, maths and physics. Captain Gray was frequently disappointed to find the morning lesson run aground on our mutual ignorance. Nonetheless he proved an excellent student, patient and bright, and we covered subjects ranging from electromagnetism to the human immune system within our first weeks. Our first project was to manufacture a pair of artificial lenses for my eyes. Learning that the doctor of the Alpaca wasn't equipped with contact lenses, I asked if the captain might bring me a pair of reading glasses. I knew from experience that, whilst they would prove useless when worn over my nose in the usual way, if they were held a certain distance from my face then a small point in the middle of the cabin would spring into focus. Once we had fitted a frame to the front of my casket I was able to instruct the captain as he made diagrams on a blackboard. From then on I learned to digest my surroundings in small but perfectly clear portions.

During my stay on the Alpaca, I was charged into the care of Hollis, the engineering cadet. Secured to a desk at the foot of his bunk, I became his pet project, a situation that reminded me of Gulliver's stay at Brobdingnag. After my lesson with the captain, Hollis fed me my first meal of the day, usually salt pork and biscuits served with beer or water (the exception being Sundays, when breakfast was skipped in anticipation of a large roast lunch). Sometimes a porpoise was caught and made into a soup. Hollis cut my pieces small with knife and fork. I felt the unsavoury food pass over my tongue and disappear down my gullet: where to, I couldn't be sure. My only clue came when I asked him to hold my casket to one of the few mirrors aboard the Alpaca. My container was built deeper than I had realised. Beneath the hinged door it extended maybe another eight inches. Perhaps I had a stomach down there? I pressed my chin to my neck, trying to see into the lower depths, but found only darkness.

The rest of Hollis's day was given to running errands for the chief engineer, shadowing any work that needed attention in the engine room, and making studies of the piston cylinders. For the majority of the afternoon I was left to listen in on the crew's production of Othello, under the direction of Father Preflogs. This was the low point of my day. The priest kept the ageing script locked in a drawer in his cabin. Unwilling to lend it out, he had personally transcribed the various parts for each cast member. This was by now unnecessary. The play had been performed so many times by the company, on beaches and brackish lagoons throughout the tropics, that all the players knew each other's lines by heart. As such, their roles had become vague and despondent. In the early weeks of rehearsal the ship's carpenter Mr Hode approached me in secret, asking on behalf of the whole cast if I could help them script something new. It turned out they had been working toward this end for months, but so far all submissions had been rejected by the priest. I took it upon myself to speak with Father Preflogs personally, explaining the need for fresh material. As the captain's library had nothing that could help, I offered to reproduce the script of the movie Highlander, a film I had seen so many times as a child, I felt confident I could remember word for word. Hollis, returning from his chores in the engine room, sounded interested. It began, I told them, with a swordfight in the carpark of a sports stadium, then quickly flashed back several hundred years through time to ancient Scotland, where a battle was being fought on the edge of a loch. Father Preflogs gave me a week to produce the script to Highlander before he resumed rehearsals for Othello.

So I became part of the crew. After my initial delight at finding a useful role on the Alpaca I soon became frustrated. It didn't take long for me to be drawn into dreary personal politics. I was carried into the crow's nests or the galleys, the stables or the stores, while my bearers complained at length about their crewmates. Occasionally I was misused.

Meanwhile Captain Gray and I were working on a science project together: a solar still. Our hogsheads of water were continually running low, and since I had presented a good case for reducing the alcohol intake of the crew, promising that health aboard ship would be dramatically improved if we halved rum rations and supplemented them with water, Mr Hode agreed to build a large conical frame which we skinned with canvas and placed over a tin bath of seawater on an unshaded part of the aftcastle. We set bowls and beakers around the edge to catch water that dripped from the cone. But for some reason, even though we were sailing through cloudless equatorial seas, by the time thirteen gallons of seawater had evaporated, we had collected less than half a pint of fresh water. To make matters worse our harvest tasted so filthy as to be almost undrinkable. Mr Hode, who was a temperate man, agreed to continue working alongside us on the project, while the rest of the crew returned to their grog. With a long writing implement we had fashioned, that I could hold in my mouth, I began drawing up plans for a new still. I knew our problems didn't stem from the design but from our choice of materials. The water must have soaked into the canvas and evaporated. I came up with an alternative plan using a pane of glass, but to my surprise found the Alpaca had none to spare.

After a little while we dropped anchor at an atoll shaped like a sock and I was taken ashore. Hollis, who wouldn't usually have been invited to join the landing party, stood astern of the skiff holding me up to see. We found the beach inhabited by a herd of cows, their bronze-painted horns being the only sign of a native presence. Second Mate Elliot shot a couple for our supper and the rest cantered off into the brushwood. Without wasting further time the group split into two. The larger half moved up the beach and began preparing an impromptu stage for our forthcoming performance of Highlander. Mr Hode, already in costume as the Kurgan, began work on a marquee. A smaller party followed the fleeing cows inland in search of vitamin C. Hollis and I stayed to perform a ferry service, travelling back and forth on the landing skiff, until only Captain Gray, First Mate Terry and a couple of crewmen remained aboard ship. As we crossed the bay we admired peach storm clouds rising over the Alpaca's masts.

Later, when the cast of Highlander had withdrawn for a private dress rehearsal, Hollis and I collected cowry shells from rock pools. He told me how once on a beach like this they had found a church entirely buried beneath the sand. Only the weathervane had given it away. When we grew bored I dared Hollis to climb one of the stacks of rock to the headland. From the top we saw pelicans riding the hot breeze over crowded lemon groves. We cheered. There were our men shaking the trees and catching lemons in sailing cloth. I suggested we might go join them, and Hollis began working carefully along the cliff with me in his satchel, until we became lost in deep vegetation. Following the cries of our nearby crewmates only seemed to lead us deeper into the vine-strangled groves. Eventually we found our way back to the group, but not before Hollis had noticed something curious. What I had mistaken for a natural feature of the rock turned out to be three full-scale statues of war planes, each carved from a single enormous boulder, which must have been rolled uphill for that purpose. Although they were half covered with creepers and tropical flowers, they showed signs of having been recently visited. We had planned to report our discovery to the crew, but when we at last rejoined them they were standing in troubled silence on a high mound. They had spotted several ships anchored on the far side of the atoll, high-castled gun-brigs flying Dutch colours. I gathered from Hollis that the Netherlands owned the trade monopoly in these waters. Had they seen us, there would certainly have been a confrontation. We ran down to the shore to gather the rest of the party and make a getaway.

Sadly, before the first skiff had brought us back to the ship, she came under attack. We heard cannon and the hiss of a salvo travelling across the bay. Chain-shot tore into the Alpaca's mainmast, severing the yardarm. There was a commotion aboard the skiff and I was dropped to the floor as the Alpaca returned fire. For some time I could see only the sky overhead and an oar being worked in the oarlock. When we were again safely aground on the beach Hollis righted my casket. The Alpaca had been seized by the Dutch. Mr Hode had seen several bodies tossed overboard, Captain Gray's among them. The men quickly fell into discussion. It was agreed that, rather than showing a flag of surrender to the enemy, we should hide ourselves ashore, hoping we had remained unnoticed, and later try to barter with the islanders. We were a large and well armed company. Together some of the men managed to drag the skiff up the beach into the maritime grass then brushed over our tracks. We made a small fire for the beef, sucked juice from the lemons and posted a lookout.

The islanders found us that evening. They marched past our hiding place in a great show of force, with painted wooden rifles at their shoulders. Second Mate Elliot led us out with his weapon pointing in the air. He quickly found the islanders' French better than their English, and switched languages, after which I couldn't follow the conversation.

We were invited back to their hamlet, a collection of some thirty dwellings built on a promontory a short way down the beach. I had half expected to be received by them as a god, but the islanders seemed to have little interest in me. While the other men were invited to eat and wash, I was set on the ground outside a sty of dwarf pigs that touched their snouts against my lens frame. Only Hollis stayed with me, interpreting the mysterious shapes bobbing around in my besmeared glasses. The first was a group of locals performing a spectacular routine on the beach that closely resembled cricket. Out to sea youngsters were practising the art of surfing on the backs of turtles. Everybody paused and saluted whenever a military procession marched past. The soldiers moved as a body, swung their left arms and stamped when they turned corners. When they came closer Hollis was able to see they had painted 'USA' on their bare chests and wooden rifles. Eventually Elliot stumbled back from the feast, bringing a bowl of nutmeg porridge with shellfish. The head islander was asking difficult questions, Elliot told us. He wondered if I might be able to help.

Again I was to be employed as an advisor. Again my knowledge of the subject was hopelessly lacking. That night I was carried to the highest point of the atoll. A gaunt woman wearing earpieces knelt down and spoke into a wooden crate. She pressed her hand to her ear as though operating a piece of radio equipment. Fires were lit in the lemon groves below. As always I took in the scene with Hollis's help. Strung between the trees were the gantries and aerials of a mock control tower woven from coconut fibre and grass. Jumbled on the scrubland I saw the long shadows of marching patrols. Occupying a clearing at the centre were more stone carvings of bomber planes and military jeeps.

Under my direction we spent the following week clearing a landing strip in the forest. When asked if we needed lighting, I said there should be small lamps placed along the runway, blue for takeoff and red for landing. Mr Hode suggested we use braziers of coal and powdered copper. Then I wondered if there shouldn't also be men standing on the ground waving green glowsticks. These were supplied by dipping firebrands in alcohol. Amazingly, on the eighth night our efforts proved successful. We heard the roar of twin engines and saw lights in the low cloud.

Minutes later an American plane, a B-25 Mitchell, appeared through the fog, lowered its landing gear and touched down on the runway. The islanders began celebrating at once, as a young pilot opened a hatch in the side of the cockpit. In fact everyone, including the former crew of the Alpaca, threw themselves into their revelry so wholeheartedly that when the American and his co-pilot jumped to the ground they were largely ignored. Once they had eventually managed to grab Mr Hode's attention, and had spoken with him for a moment or two, I saw them pointing in my direction. The pilots pushed their way through the celebrating crowd until they reached Hollis, who was happily spinning me around in circles. We stopped dancing when we saw how serious the pilots looked. They peered into my casket. 'We're looking for someone who can tell us about quantum entanglement' said the co-pilot.

Clare Wallace

Clare Wallace was born in Cambridge in 1982. She first attempted short stories on the Creative Writing MA at Bath Spa University. On the MA she made some invaluable friends who she still meets once a month for a writing workshop. Earlier this year she reached the final 50 in the *Mslexia Women's Short Story Competition*. This is her first, but hopefully not her last, work of published fiction. Currently she is writing as much as she can and seeking work experience in the publishing industry. Clare lives in Cardiff and is owned by a cow-patterned cat called Moo.

But Then Again, Maybe it is

I go out looking for my girlfriend with my dog. All over Cardiff. That's what we do. Not going to give up until we find her. Anyway, dogs need a good yomp about - got to keep them fit see.

We got a dog instead of having a baby. My girlfriend said it was what people do as a trial, to see if they're ready, you know, to look after something helpless. 'Maybe we should start with a goldfish,' my girlfriend said. But you can't cwtch a goldfish.

We named him after Jeff Buckley. Maybe that was where we went wrong, naming him after a dead musician. Maybe we shouldn't have got a mongrel either. Maybe we should have paid a daft fee to have a dog with good breeding. Maybe then he wouldn't have left a shit in my girlfriend's slippers. Mind you, judging by the two of us, I'm not sure our kid would have had good breeding either - might have been a right little bugger. But I wouldn't have cared. I would have loved it anyway. Of course I would. Love this bloody dog silly, I do. My mam says I treat it better than I do most people, but that's not true, I don't reckon. But then again, maybe it is. Most people, in my experience, don't deserve niceness because they just take from you and never give anything back - nothing worth having anyway. You only got to watch the news once to know that. But dogs, they don't ask for anything. They just gives.

Buckley sounds like a dog's name, too, don't it? We was wondering about Dylan or Lennon or Lou, but none of them suited him right. We both agreed on Buckley. It was a joint decision. Everything is supposed to be joint, isn't it? Bank accounts, mortgages, dressing gowns. My girlfriend was always robbing my dressing gown. I didn't mind; it always smelt better when she'd been in it.

Music was the one great thing my mam give me. She used to work from home, my mam, and she'd put records on so I didn't have to hear her or the associates that was visiting.

Music is what my girlfriend and me have in common. She's got a stunning voice my girlfriend. She used to sing and I used to play the guitar. She's got a voice like that first sip of whisky; perfect and warming, and straight to your chest. We liked all the gloomy songs, we did. Suckers for heartbreak. At night we'd put a blanket on the floor and lie down. We'd drink and smoke, listening to all our favourite songs in the dark. She'd hold my hand and sometimes she'd cry. If it was raining, we'd have the windows open; we liked the mud smell and we didn't care about the wet coming in. 'What's a bit of water when you've got rain in your heart?' my girlfriend said, snuggled under my arm.

It's not too late; that's what Jeff Buckley said. My kingdom for a kiss on her shoulder. My blood for her laughter. That's proper love, that is; the kind that nearly kills you.

OK, so the truth is I stole Buckley and smuggled him home. Took him from some gypos outside town. I had a squint as I walked past their caravans, and they had him tied up. Poor pup kept on one shoddy piece of grass; I should've burnt the place to the ground. They're lucky I didn't.

My girlfriend said I was all talk, she said I never did the things I promised, like paint the kitchen and tidy up my side of the bedroom. Like get a job and stop drinking. She made it sound like it was easy. And, don't get me wrong, I'd have a potch about and put my clothes away or stack up the CDs or get the mugs from under the bed and give them a swill, but painting the kitchen was a huge big job. It involves dosh for a start to buy the paint with and before that you've got to decide on a colour. I didn't mind the yellow walls; I thought they was quite summery, but my girlfriend said they was more of a pus shade. She'd go on and on about it, her voice like an ant crawling round my ear. And I'd have a gutsful and say, 'All right; I'll do it now; in a minute.' But I didn't. She'd watch some crappy design show with a pair of poofs chopsing about laminate flooring and spotlights and she'd say, 'Look at that; glam-oh-rus.' Drove me nuts that did. Glam-oh-rus. 'Ain't that swanky?' she'd say, 'I never seen anything as swanky as that.'

She done her best to make the place pretty, though. She put flowers in a vase on the kitchen table. But she put any old thing in there. 'That's a summery yellow,' she'd say, pointing at a glass full of dandelions. But I loved that about her. She liked things most people didn't. Fortunate for me that she did.

Pale blue eyes she had, like the Lou Reed song. Linger on them I did. I could look at those eyes forever, and I told her so. My mountain top. Everything I've had but couldn't keep.

OK, so the truth is I stole Buckley when I was supposed to be at a job interview. I was on my way and there he was, yipping and yapping, and looking proper lonely. It was a terrible job anyway. Selling kitchen electricals. Flogging poppity pings. Give you cancer them things. I'm sure of it. Not ethical, are they? All that radioactivity. Can't do a job I don't believe in. If you're going to sell your soul it should be for something that will make you a legend, like Robert Johnson.

Right now I'd sell my soul to have my girlfriend back. My girlfriend was working in a bar when we met. I stopped in for a pint. She was married but nearly divorced, like the Dylan song. Helped her out of a bit of bother I did but I used too much of my fist. Broke my hand on her ex-husband's face. He wouldn't stop harassing her; kept hanging around - making her feel unsafe. I thought Buckley might help with that, too. You know, make her feel safer. Wanted to protect her, honestly I did; wanted to marry her, have babies, have a family with her and Buckley. But we was tangled up in blue. Both of us. She said I wasn't good for her, that I was sad enough for the both of us, and she was sad enough on her own.

OK, so the truth is I stopped for a whisky before the job interview, just for a bit of courage. Had a mooch about the town after that, looking in a jeweller's window and wishing I could get my girlfriend an engagement ring - a proper big sparkler. I think about my girlfriend all the day, see. Thought a ring might show her I was serious. I thought about what she'd said about how we wasn't ready for a baby, and I near broke into tears then, staring at that shop window. That's what got me thinking about a dog.

OK, so the truth is I didn't take Buckley from some gypos. I took him from some kids in the park, but they weren't looking after him properly because he was tied to a slide ladder and they were on the swings, and he was yipping and yapping and looking lonely. There was no proof they weren't gypos; might have been for all I knew. Buckley came with me happy enough; trotted after me, good as gold, and I reckon he chose who he wanted to be with. He's got these eyes like a baby seal, big and black, like a love potion them eyes. Even my girlfriend couldn't say no to them. She tried though.

OK, so the truth is my girlfriend had really had enough when I came home that day with the dog and smelling of booze, and the job centre having rung about me missing the interview. We had a stonker of a row that night, but we did it all in whispers because of Buckley. Hissing at each other we was. We can't have an unfriendly atmosphere like this, I explained, not if we're going to have a dog. They pick up on these things, and we don't want an anxious yapper who jumps at the sound of his own backdoor breeze.

My girlfriend looked like she was about to lamp me one. 'Why do you do this?' she said. But Buckley made a wuff noise and looked at us both with his head tilted. Well, we tried to keep our faces cross but Buckley was having none of it, he laid on his back, wiggling his belly, and then we were both on the floor rubbing it and stroking his ears and taking turns to lift him up and cwtch him. Pure magic. Good day sunshine, that's what it felt like, them Beatles knew what they were talking about. My girlfriend went straight out and bought a lead and then we were off walking along the Taff, loving each other again, lying beneath a shady tree while Buckley rollicked around and there was me feeling like the proudest luckiest fella anywhere.

Could mention something about not letting the sun go down on me, but I've always thought Elton John was a bit of a prat; so did my girlfriend, except for the song about the tidy dancer - she liked that one. Anyway, I mean the day had to end didn't it. Can't be sunshine all the time.

My mam used to say, 'Don't go breaking your legs and come running to me.'

OK, so the truth is that my girlfriend saw the reward poster with a sort of description of me on it and a photo of Buckley. Taped all over the lampposts. They were going to give £200 for Buckley's return. But he was ours by then. 'Why do you do this?' my girlfriend said again.

One day - and this was the beginning of the end, this was - my girlfriend came home and Buckley had trashed the place. There was the shit in her slippers, the beanbags were ripped and spilling everywhere, there was a bottle of wine knocked over, CDs all over the floor, her clothes all over the bedroom, mangled and torn. 'I've had enough,' she said. 'It's me or the dog.' And I thought that she'd calm down, so I took Buckley out for a yomp, let him run it off a little bit. And, when I got back to the house, there she was, gone.

Haven't seen her since. We waited a week, not going anywhere, just sitting there, me and Buckley, listening to records and clock-watching. But the dog biscuits ran out and so did the glug. Joni Mitchell made me go to the shops. Didn't even like her that much, but my girlfriend did. Joni made my girlfriend close her eyes and say, 'That's singing, that is. Don't that make you wistful?' You got to keep thinking you can make it through the waves, Joni said. There's sinking everywhere. So me and Buckley took to the streets and started looking for my girlfriend, determined to stay afloat we was.

OK, so the truth is my girlfriend didn't believe for a second it was the dog who trashed the place. 'Why's the guitar not touched then?' she said. The wine, the beanbags, the clothes, the CDs: it was all me. Although the dog did shit in her slippers. She said I was the worst liar she ever saw. 'Lies,' she said. 'All you got is other people's words.'

'That's all any of us have got,' I said.

I'd been down the pub, see, and I thought I saw her walk past with someone, thought I saw her kissing a man at the traffic lights by the castle. I squinted and realised it wasn't her, but on the way home I was imagining it, because I'd felt it, and the pain was burning up inside me. By the time I got back to the flat I was fuming, smoking with rage; I was all raw temper.

I tried to play her John Lennon. 'I'm a jealous guy,' I said.

'You don't listen,' she said.

'Listen here,' I said. 'I lost control, but I didn't mean to hurt nobody.'

She said she couldn't bear me no more, that she felt sorry for a dog like Buckley being stuck with a miserable drunk like me. She said if I wasn't careful I'd end up on the streets, with nothing but Buckley to keep me warm, and she said that Buckley deserved better than that. She told me to leave while she got her stuff together.

'You're the other half of my sky,' I said. 'My life is in your hands. Yoko and John,' I said, 'they had trying times but they stayed together.'

'Get out,' she said.

Hello darkness my old butty. Silence grows like a tumour. That's why I prefer to be out looking. It's never quiet in town. Never. Even at five in the morning there are people about. People who might know where my girlfriend is. 'Leave her alone if she don't want to be found,' my mam says. 'You can't find something if it's not there.'

'You don't know what love is,' my girlfriend said. John Lennon said love is wanting to be loved. My mam says love was invented by chocolate companies and florists. A card in the newsagents says love is knowing when to say you're sorry. I'd like to tell my girlfriend I'm sorry.

Truth is, my girlfriend might not be in Cardiff anymore. Can't stop looking for her though. Sometimes I don't even make it home. Me and Buckley just fall down somewhere, or I fall down and Buckley waits with me until I wake up.

Life is very long when you're lonely. The Smiths said that. All the lonely people, where do they come from? The Beatles said that. They was right to ask. At least I got Buckley.

Acknowledgments

Bristol Short Story Prize is extremely fortunate to receive support and help from numerous people, the majority of which is offered voluntarily. BSSP would like to thank the following for their invaluable contributions:

Our readers – Sophie Collard, Katherine Hanks, Lu Hersey, Richard Jones, Mike Manson, Dawn Pomroy, Ali Reynolds and Keith Taylor; this year's judges – Bertel Martin (chair), Joe Berger, Maia Bristol, Helen Hart and Tania Hershman ; Chris Hill, Jonathan Ward, Gaby Selby and the 3rd year Illustration students at University of the West of England; John Bennett and the Year 10 art students at Henbury School; Nick Bright, Tom Farrant and Jess Stephens at Filton College; and Peter Begen, Joe Burt, Mark Furneval, Ellen Grant, Zoe Hall, Fran Ham, Nicky Johns, Sylvie Kruiniger, Nick Law, Marc Leverton, Miranda Lewis, Kathy McDermott, Robin McDowell, Catherine Mason, Peter Morgan, Dave Oakley, Caroline Pettifer, Sarah Salway, John Sansom, Joshua Tallent and Chris Woollatt.